The Arms of God

Also by Lynne Hinton

FICTION

Friendship Cake

Hope Springs

Forever Friends

The Things I Know Best

The Last Odd Day

NONFICTION

Meditations for Walking

The Arms of God

A NOVEL

Lynne Hinton

St. Martin's Press New York

 For information, address St. Martin's Press, 175 Fifth Avenue, New York, N.Y. 10010.

www.stmartins.com

Library of Congress Cataloging-in-Publication Data

Hinton, J. Lynne.
The arms of God : a novel / Lynne Hinton.—1st ed.
p. cm.
ISBN 0-312-34795-2
EAN 978-0-312-34795-6
1. Parent and adult child—Fiction. 2. Mothers and daughters—Fiction. 3. Maternal deprivation—Fiction. 4. Abandoned children—Fiction. 5. Loss (Psychology)—Fiction. I. Title.

PS3558.I457A89 2005
813'.54—dc22

2005046567

First Edition: November 2005

10 9 8 7 6 5 4 3 2 1

FOR MY HUSBAND, BOB BRANARD,

LIGHT OF MY LIFE,

KEEPER OF MY DREAMS

ACKNOWLEDGMENTS

The writer's path bears surprising curves, steep hills, and unexpected delays. I faced a difficult part of my journey when I was released from my former publisher. It was a stretch of disappointment for which I was unprepared. During that time of facing my losses, trying to regroup, and setting out again, I was cared for and supported by many dear souls. I am most grateful for my agent and my friend, Sally McMillan, who pulled me up and through those dark days. I have a husband whose love never wavered even when I was so much less than loveable. I had constant attention from those friends and family members who kept encouraging me to keep walking and to keep writing. Thank you to everyone who journeyed with me during that year.

Finally, I headed in a new direction when Linda McFall of St. Martin's Press offered me a place to share my stories. Thank you, Linda, for taking a chance on me. Thank you to the people at St. Martin's for giving this book its voice.

I gratefully acknowledge that my life is blessed, that this writer's path, though difficult at times, is still the only path I would choose, and though there have been more than a few lonesome hours, there has never been a part of this journey where I have had to walk alone.

Once in a while when the earth comes cold
you'll spot a place of sun;
and before your eyes can look away
the rest of you will run
straight into that blast of red
that is someone's angry pain;
you'll stand for just a second
and warm, remember her again.

—ES

The Arms of God

Prologue

Olivia is dead. I was shelling peas when the phone rang. Thinking about Anna and her fight with the little Thompson boy. Remembering how troublesome the world can be to a ten-year-old girl. Wondering what her father might have told her. Smiling that we got through the Thompson boy crisis just like all the others without hand or handout from the person she used to call Daddy. Thinking about the man next door, Richard, Rick, and how the swamp maple tree in the front yard grew ripe with red flowers early, the first day of spring, the day he moved in. Thinking about shelling peas and how my fingers were going to be stained. Blue-green like the bruise under Anna's eye.

Anna has her grandmother's eyes. Brown as the earth. Dark with a light and a sadness both at the same time. A riverbed of muddied gladness with an unexpected appreciation for grief. I knew they were familiar the first time I fell into them; but I didn't know why until I dropped down again into the other pair, the older pair, when I opened my front door to the old woman standing on my porch three weeks ago.

She waited there, lost and found, broken and set, the sun balanced across her shoulders; and I saw her mark upon my daughter when she lifted up her head and swallowed me up with that vision. I knew and didn't know, fell and got back up, all at the same time.

I had been in the kitchen that day too. It was Saturday and I was capping late strawberries, making freezer jam. I was pleased with myself, finding the time to go to Murray's Patch, pick a couple of gallons of ripe berries, sort and clean them, and then make the breakfast syrup that Anna loves to pour over her biscuits. I was planning to take a quart to Rick, an easy way of thanking him for fixing the leak underneath the house, an innocent means of seeing him again. When the doorbell rang my hands were sticky and I was smiling; and I pulled the door open using my elbows, my lips stretched across my teeth. I think I must have hoped for company.

And there she was. And there were those eyes, those eyes of my child now set into the face of an old woman. And there was the flood of memory.

It was no more than a split second of time, a moment moving forward and back, crashing together. And I realized just in the wake of the news of her death that it was in that split second that it happened. Something too familiar to be a dream stared up at me and broke through a wall that had been built across the low corners of my mind.

The movement was as quick as lightning and just as red-hot. It swirled into that sticky-fingered second and I found myself falling down into a time long forgotten, a time held away and squeezed aside; and I blinked hard and circled, emptying myself into a one-worded question of "Yes?"

Trying to forget where those eyes had taken me. Trying to act like nothing had slipped and fallen. Trying to forget that the lost memories and the hopes of a child could settle down deep beneath the heart of a woman and be raised up so quickly by just a glance. Trying to pretend to myself and to this familiar stranger that I never harbored an ache or that I recognized the eyes; and rather it was only a tiny lapse of imagination that shifted the thick barricade of bricks that had been stacked hard against my secrets. Trying to return to the order of a woman standing on my front porch and the bloodlike glaze dripping from my fingers.

I pulled up the apron and wiped my hands, the door resting against my left hip. I neither moved near her nor retreated. I only watched and waited as she pushed a piece of hair from her face, placing it behind her ear, delicate, like a girl in love, and then finally whispered my name as if it were the medicine she needed for pain. And when she looked up again, having dropped her face and then lifted her eyes again to me, I knew even then that her dying could do nothing to me like her coming did. So that is why I was surprised when I hung up the phone after the call from the emergency-room doctor and found that a tear had moistened my lip.

I took my time getting to the hospital. I straightened up the kitchen as I sorted through the details of what was passing over me. I threw out the hulls, put the peas in a tight plastic bag, setting them on the shelf in the refrigerator. I wiped down the table and even washed the bowls. Then I dried and placed them on the lazy Susan after I rearranged the other plastic containers that were unstacked and in disarray, glad to have the opportunity to take care of the task I had put aside for months. I emptied out the dishwater and cleaned out the sink with 409 and a sponge. Then I swept the floor, the broom pulled across every space, reaching into corners and under cabinets. I almost decided to mop but then thought better of it.

The truth was I did not want to go to her bedside. I did not desire the role of family member to a dead woman. I did not want to fill out the forms and sign the papers. After all, I had only just met my mother twenty days before, only just learned how to call her name and what time she was accustomed to eating her meals, what afternoon of the week we might expect her to drop by and how carefully she chose her words.

I was completely unprepared with how to be in control of her belongings, how to label her dying, how to finish her life. And I wondered as I slid the dirt and hulls and strings into the dustpan and then threw them into the trash can, how does a daughter claim the lost body of a forgotten parent, plan a service of remembrance, act bereaved when the reunion had only barely begun?

How does a child tell the doctor the medical history she doesn't know? Respond with the appropriate grief and sadness? Know exactly which church to call, what hopeful songs to sing, and what death clothes to dress her in? I'd think of one question and five more would follow. So I spent another thirty minutes going through the kitchen, arranging boxes and bowls in the pantry and cabinets, and then finally calling Rick to ask him if he'd stay with Anna when she got home from her soccer practice.

"You okay?" he asked, after answering that he would be happy to babysit. I could hear the music in the background, the oldies station playing some Beach Boys tune. I closed my eyes and could see the calm light in his smile, feel the gentle sweep of his fingers across the back of my neck.

"I don't know," I responded.

There was a pause. He waited.

"Do you want me to explain anything to Anna?" he asked. I could hear him turn the volume down on his radio.

I hadn't thought about telling Anna. I hadn't considered how I would explain this to her.

"No," I said. "Just say that I had an important errand to run. I'll tell her about it later."

He hesitated again. "I'm sorry," he said. "I know this has been confusing for you."

And I took a breath, remembering the way I had stumbled over an explanation for who Olivia was when he dropped by one evening while she was visiting.

"It's complicated," I told him the next day as we stood inside the row of dogwood trees that bordered our properties. "I haven't seen or heard from my mother in a very long time." The sunlight danced through the full and tender branches stretching around us.

"All families are complicated," he said and he reached behind my ear and pulled a narrow limb close to my face, a fine white flower falling below my eyes. He held it there, letting the petals rest against the bridge of my nose, and then he let the limb loose. It snapped gently back in place. Then he smiled and we had not spoken of Olivia again.

"Thanks, Rick," I said and we hung up.

I drove to the hospital thinking about my daughter and how I would tell her of her grandmother's passing and remembered the other conversation I had trying to explain about my mother, the one I had with Anna after Olivia ate dinner with us for the first time.

"Miss Olivia is your mother?" she asked.

I hummed the answer while I paid bills at the kitchen table. I was using the calculator. I was wearing my glasses.

"How come I never saw her before?"

"I don't know," I said, trying not to be distracted from the task at hand, trying not to get tangled in a ten-year-old's line of questioning, trying not to ask myself the same thing.

"You haven't seen her in a long time?"

"No, not for a long time." The electric bill was high for a spring season. I punched in the number, watching my checking account dwindle.

I felt Anna staring at me. I felt her eyes, her pity. I sighed, knowing the hard one was coming.

"Where's she been all this time?"

I pulled off my glasses and slid the chair away from the table. I dropped my hands in my lap. I breathed in and I breathed out. I closed my eyes and opened them. I turned toward my daughter and answered her. "Anna, I don't know."

And my ten-year-old child, the daughter bearing such a resemblance to her newly arrived grandmother, the one who had delivered me from loneliness a decade earlier, the one who did not flinch from truth, nodded like she understood.

She jumped down from the countertop where she had been sitting, patted me on my arm like she was suddenly the grown-up, and then, like Rick, didn't ask anything else. She went into the den to watch television while I sat alone with what had and had not been revealed. I sat alone with the only story I knew to tell but didn't.

In the summer when I was four Olivia walked with me on a Tuesday to Miss Kathy's Play Care Center, the big white house with a fenced-in yard, where I stayed every weekday while she worked. I did not take note that the day was starting out differently from any other day. It was Tuesday and that meant swim day, bologna sandwich day, and that Miss Kathy's daughter, having worked the late shift on Monday night, would still be sleeping when we arrived. We began every Tuesday morning playing quietly outside.

I had not noticed Olivia's red puffy eyes or the long desperate way she hugged me at the door. I had not asked about the bag of my clothes that she left behind the coat tree or the five dollars she pinned inside the front zippered pocket of my blue striped overalls. I had not determined anything curious or different about my mother. I left her side and ran to the backyard where three or four other children were already playing.

The sun was rising, high and hot, and Miss Kathy was wearing her green dress, the one with tiny yellow flowers that danced like bees across her chest every time she moved. Through the window in the door I watched her walk away from the sink, drying her hands as she spoke to my mother, and I imagined there was the sound of humming following her, the sounds I had heard in ripe, full gardens.

Olivia raised her hand, a kiss gently placed upon her fingers and then sent to me with a smile like she did every morning. I waved back and then forgot her, simply and easily forgot her, thinking only of having my turn on the tire swing that Miss Kathy's husband had hung from the fat arm of the cottonwood tree and wishing it was already time to swim.

I did not worry that anything was wrong late in the afternoon when everyone else left, mothers grinning and waiting for their children at the curb or on the porch. I did not peer from the front window or stay seated near the door. The sun dropped and I still did not become upset. After supper I spent the night watching cartoons and eating ice cream with Miss Kathy's daughter while her mother watched from the table in the kitchen, her face pinched and bothered. I fell asleep on the sofa in the den, listening to the whispers and finally starting to feel only slightly concerned that something was not right.

The following afternoon when the two police officers arrived and the skinny lady in a tight blue suit asked me if my mother had said anything to me about where she might have gone, I still did not believe that things were any different than they had been for the first four years of my life.

Even as I rode away, sitting in the front seat of a squad car, the other children watching from Miss Kathy's front yard, tops of heads and tight plump fingers lining the fence, I did not consider that my mother was never coming back. I thought it was only a misunderstanding, a mistake that would quickly be remedied, that things were as they should be. I was, after all, only four; I had not yet made space in my life for gross disappointment. Little did I understand how unsettled I would soon become bearing the consequences of the occasion of my mother's disappearance. Little did I know how unsorted my life was about to be.

The hospital was not far from the house where Anna and I lived. It was a big sprawling building with lots of informational signs. There was a visitors parking garage, two lots for day patients and staff, and a small designated lot for the emergency department that was tucked behind the new cancer center, marked with large red letters. I knew which side of the hospital it was on because of the few times I had taken Anna. A high temperature, a twisted ankle, a rash from some kind of poison, we had made our rounds to Saint Vincent's.

Once when Anna was a baby, John had gone with me. Anna had developed a cough, deep and raspy like an old smoker. It was croup; and together John and I stayed with her, he and I drinking cups of black coffee and nibbling on vending machine snacks while Anna slept fitfully beneath an oxygen tent.

He was a husband then, to me, not to the college coed he now lived with on the edge of town. He was a father to Anna, doting and concerned, tearful and guilt-ridden that he might have caused her illness because he had not wrapped her in her blanket on the night we sat and counted the stars. He was not yet distracted and busy by his teaching obligations or wrapped up in the life of another woman. He loved me then but he left me too, just like my mother.

His departure was just as quick, just as premeditated; but unlike hers, I knew he was leaving. From the very beginning of our marriage I was ready for his disappearance. I knew he would go.

That was the trickiest part of Olivia's leaving. That has been the thing I have never set loose. Once I realized what had happened, once I understood the permanence of what had occurred, that I had grown up without her, I simply expected that my mother was only the first of many departures.

I assumed that since she had left me, that since she had packed me a bag and given me five dollars, that since she had made a plan to drop me off at Miss Kathy's and never come back, that everyone else was making a way to leave me too. I'm still haunted by trying to figure out who's going next, how my daughter will also one day soon fall away, how Rick, even though he bears no resemblance to my ex-husband, will also follow the growing line of those checking out of my life.

I walked slowly from the parking lot to the entrance, the sliding-glass doors opening as I stood just under the overhang. There was an older woman at the front desk. She was talking on the phone, the receiver at her ear. I waited politely. She slipped the mouthpiece down past her chin and said, "I'll be with you in just a minute."

She was nice enough; but I could feel her sizing me up, taking in the clues as to whether I was sick or hurt, whether I would pay for the visit or be the next charity case. She studied me while she listened to the person on the other end of the phone.

"Yes, the mouse is stuck. I can't turn it on, can't turn it off," she explained.

It was computer problems. From my own work as a secretary at the business office at the college I knew the symptoms. Finally, after telling this a few times to first one person, then another, she hung up.

"Computers," she said, "can't live with them, can't shoot them!"

I smiled, trying to think of something sympathetic or witty to say in response but knowing I had nothing to offer her.

"Now," she exhaled, "how can I help you?" She pulled out a clipboard and began preparing the forms.

"I was called." I was hesitant in my reply. "Olivia Jacobs?" I asked, in hopes she would need no more explanation.

She pursed her lips and crossed her brow. She had forgotten the dead woman who had been pushed against a corner in the last examining room. She had forgotten that they were waiting for the daughter, that the chaplain had come and gone, two, maybe three times, that the doctor who declared the woman dead had already left for the day.

"Ah," she said, remembering. "Let me call the nurse."

Then I felt her judge me again. Me, the family member,

alone to see the dead mother. She was assessing my grief, deciding whether to page the chaplain, whether I was a weeper or a runner, potential trouble for the emergency-room staff.

Hospital personnel hate weepers and runners, this I learned from overhearing a conversation of nurses while I waited for Anna's X-ray when she was seven and turned her ankle chasing a neighbor's dog.

"Weepers are trouble for everybody," one nurse explained to another, "and one can never be sure where a runner will run." There was a tired sort of laughter that followed and I quit listening when the doctor walked in with the long black picture of my daughter's bones.

I put on my best face as the receptionist continued to measure me. This, I have learned, is a gift.

After Olivia left me, I was placed in an emergency foster home and then later moved to a regular one. I lived with seven families from the time I was four until the time I was fifteen. Then I lived in a group home for teenage girls until I graduated from high school. I kept my clothes in a suitcase, my toys and other belongings in a bag, even when I was told which dresser drawers were mine and which side of the closet I could hang my things.

I learned how to adapt to families who prayed at every meal and read the Bible and homeschooled the children as well as to families where you understood how to live carefully, with caution, how never to be alone with certain male adults. I learned how to get along with mean, selfish girls and what pleases but does not overwhelm the parents. I learned how to eat foods I had never before tasted and how to drink milk without getting sick. I figured things out quickly and by myself. I knew how to put on my best face.

The nurse who came to walk me to the room where the dead woman lay was young and pretty. She wore a bright pink lab coat over a perfectly starched uniform. Her teeth were white and straight, her lips painted the same color as her nails, which were short and square. Her hair had been twisted into a fine knot that gathered at the nape of her neck. Blond strands highlighted the otherwise thick brown hair; and she was tall and slender, a woman who wore confidence as if it were born on her.

"It must be hard to lose your mother," she said smoothly. The line was well rehearsed and spoken with just the right amount of sympathy and concern.

I nodded obediently as I followed her down the hall, wondering the entire way about which time she meant. I thought about the word "lose," as in "lose your mother." I thought of how it was a word that described my feelings for much of my childhood because for years I had thought that Olivia had been lost. I believed that she had been on her way back to find me, but that something had happened, a car wreck, a misdirected day trip, something spoiling her routine, and that she had gotten lost.

My greatest fear, then, in moving from house to house, in changing my address, my new family's last name, was that when she finally recovered herself and the way she was going, when she finally was no longer lost and knew she needed to pick me up, that she would not be able to find me. That then she would certainly be lost for good.

"Is there somebody I can call for you?" the pretty young nurse asked.

I noticed that her name was Heather. Heather Allan. I read it on the identification badge she wore clipped to her lapel. All the pretty girls were named Heather when I was a child. Heather and Dawn and Jennifer. My name is Alice. Worn-out and borrowed like a forgotten tool in a shed. Alice never wins a beauty pageant. Alice is never homecoming queen or head cheerleader. Alice is never called on for dates.

I had always wanted to know where Olivia had gotten such a name for a baby girl, a name already old; but I was too young to think of it before she left and too lost to it when she came back.

Growing up without any stories of an Alice, a headstrong and bold best friend from high school, a favorite aunt who married a younger man, a movie star, glamorous and mysterious, I had become the only Alice I knew to be. I was as weary as the name.

I shook my head. I liked the way she talked to me even though she treated me as if I were younger than she. I liked the sweetness, the kindness she offered. It felt nice to have someone concerned about me since I recognized a long time ago that I live my life just out of reach of most people.

"Then I'll leave you here alone with your mother," she replied.

She touched me on the shoulder, lightly, not too intimately, but with a certain degree of familiarity. She pulled the curtain around us and walked quietly to the outside door and I suddenly found myself feeling awkward and unsure of what I should now say or do to the dead woman I met and remembered but did not know. I heard Heather clear her throat. Perhaps, I thought, she was waiting for a reply; but just as I had been with the receptionist and her frozen computer I could think of nothing else to say. I had no words for death and only a few memories.

When I was six I had a special friend at the foster home named Crocus. She said her mother named her that because she had suddenly appeared like the spring flower in the dead of winter and that her mother had been so happy to see something new and alive in her life that she had named her the only flower she loved.

Crocus was fourteen and she had lived in foster homes since her mother died when she was eight. Her father, she had reported during our first conversation, had never seen his daughter; and she had never known how he looked.

She was smart and easy to be with. She taught me how to take care of myself and how to manage in the homes of others.

"The real children will never accept you," she said one day after the daughter of the foster parents told her mother I stole from her. "Just stay as far away from them and their things as you can. It'll save you a lot of trouble."

I always thought that phrase "real children" had seemed odd

when Crocus used it. But it didn't take long before I understood the difference between the biological children of the foster parents and those of us who were let in because of charity or the need for a little extra household money. Most of the time the adults tried to keep things even among us, squared up and balanced; but it was always clear and definite among the children who belonged and who didn't.

Crocus and I never belonged.

One day in winter everyone had gone out. It was one of the real children's birthdays so there was quite a celebration planned. I was sick with fever and flu and Crocus was assigned to stay home and take care of me. She kept a cold wet cloth on my brow, my glass filled with orange juice, and talked to me about what she planned to do when she lived on her own. She was going to be a marine biologist and swim carelessly through the caves and coral in the oceans. She wanted to break the record for holding her breath underwater and she told me how it felt to her when she dove deep into the pool at the community center, breaking the water for the first time.

"It's like being born," she said, a smile warming her face as she remembered the gift of summer, and then she talked about her experience with death.

I closed my eyes and listened. My breath, heavy and hot, was the only thing that stirred from within me. I was as silent as a grave.

"I have always felt I would be alone," she confessed. "Even before she died."

I knew she was speaking about her mother.

She talked on, her voice so perfectly soothing. "When I saw her for the first time after she was dead, I was brought into the room at the funeral home with all of her family, most of whom I had never met. There must have been thirty people in there and I remember that they all hushed when my grandmother took me to her casket. I remember thinking that they shouldn't be there, that they didn't have the right to grieve my mother's death, that they shouldn't be standing around watching us while I told her good-bye. That what was happening was private and personal, just for us, and that they should leave."

She dipped the cloth in a pan of water and then again draped it across my head. I settled into her story, the wet compress covering my eyes.

"But even in the midst of all those people, all those eyes staring at me, I decided that they couldn't really see us." I felt her hand press my brow. "I became a dark figure passing under a wave. And me and my mother, even in a room of people pretending to be family, watching us like they cared, we were together in the cold and bottomless sea, we were alone to ourselves."

I fell asleep to the sound of a daughter's voice rocking me in and out of a fever, her memories of death, her story of living underwater. And I dreamed of fishing for my mother from a long wooden pier. I stood as bold and clearheaded as I had ever been. I was sure I could hook her with a strong, sturdy line.

"You just come find me when you're finished." The voice of Nurse Heather was behind me. She closed the outside door, pulling me back to the moment at hand, the moment of Olivia, the moment of dealing with her passing. The curtain swung and fell and it was as still as winter.

The room at the end of the hall in the emergency department was cold and without too much light. The far and side walls were thick, painted pale green, hardly masking the heaviness of the concrete; and though I had never been in one before, gave the feeling of being in a morgue. Silver instruments lined a table built into the wall that stood next to a cabinet with glass doors. Inside the case there were jars of cotton and boxes of bandages neatly displayed in rows.

Three IV poles were pushed into a corner; and stacks of white linen and blue dotted gowns were neatly folded and placed on shelves next to the gurney. I stepped closer to the body. She was so still and calmed, so different from the tiny woman who crept into my life like a stray cat, wild and alone.

She seemed older somehow, the gray in her skin enhanced by the white sterile sheet upon which she lay. She wore no makeup and displayed no shifting of facial features that give a person some animated youthfulness. There were no black lines drawn across the lids of her eyes, no rosy pink circles highlighting her cheeks. No smooth paint slowly applied to her thin lips, which in moments of disconcerting silence that often fell between us, she anxiously bit and slid behind the backs of her teeth.

The gown hung loosely about her shoulders with sleeves, meant to be short, draped wide about her elbows. I thought how ready she looked for some news or some different face to greet her, how she had been caught waiting, and how she had finally sunk into the frame that supported her, melting into the whiteness of the fabric that held her in. Her peppered black hair spread across the pillow, still catching light and holding it like a person wide-eyed and alive.

But Olivia was dead. She was lifeless, void of breath and memory, bereft of spirit. She had left everything she had known and been while living on the earth. Everything she had learned and treasured, everyone she had touched and been touched by, every collected and cherished moment when she counted herself as alive, was gone. And she was now completely and fully absent from it all.

I suppose I thought I'd see only sorrow and disappointment in the face of Olivia, that look of regret. But as I stepped closer to the dead woman's body, taking her long wiry fingers into mine, I recognized relief.

Gone was the brittle edge of unknowingness that kept her jumpy and anxious. Missing was the quiet way she wore sadness, always close to the surface of a smile. No longer did she seem remorseful and broken, ashamed of something she never named, leaving me maybe. She was free of the mysterious past and relieved of what seemed to be a burdensome present. She no longer faced some unknown and tempestuous future. And although I hadn't had a lot of experience studying dead people, Olivia certainly appeared to be at peace. She drew in a breath, still waiting, and politely death had arrived. She looked comfortable in its presence.

Of course, I didn't have a lot of memories to compare Olivia's appearance to since the only other dead person I ever saw was Mrs. Pickett, the old foster mother I stayed with when I lived out on a farm. I was thirteen. There were five other children, two of them adopted, the other three fosters, a caretaker, Mr. Henry, who lived behind the house in the barn and only came around for Sunday dinner, and Mrs. Pickett's retarded sister named Miss Lucy. I never asked about Mr. Pickett.

Mrs. Pickett was nice enough. She was the best cook of any of the mothers I lived with. She was soft all over like biscuit dough and she had kind eyes. She adopted the two children when they were just babies and she took in foster children because she had been an orphan herself. "Back in the old hard days," she would tell us, "when all the children lived together in a long, cold warehouse they called a dormitory."

She would tell us lots of stories about how they worked from early in the morning until late at night, how they were taught never to speak unless they were spoken to and even then with only simple replies, and how none of the children ever had anything that was their own. No toy, no dress, no pair of shoes, not even their undergarments were theirs to keep.

"If you got attached to anything," she'd tell us as she took us shopping, "the principal, Mr. Blackwell, would take it away from you." She bought every child who lived with her two sets of clothes, one for church and parties, the other for school.

"The first thing I did when I got out of that orphanage was buy myself a pair of black patent boots and a tiny doll with long silk hair."

We all knew the story and even knew where she kept the little doll, high on a shelf in the living room. She took it down sometimes for us to hold. "Every child should have at least one thing that's theirs." And she'd smile with satisfaction at all the stuff she bought us.

Mrs. Pickett left the orphanage when she was eighteen. She found her sister in the hospital wing of the dormitory, tied to a bed. She wouldn't tell any of Miss Lucy's stories, only that nobody should have to live through what her sister did.

Mrs. Pickett died from a stroke, the social worker told us. And suddenly, all five children and Miss Lucy were wards of the state. Nobody could find Mr. Henry when she died. The barn was swept clean and all his things were gone. The preacher from the church where she took us had a special service just for the children. And we all went up to her casket, one by one, while he helped us say a prayer.

They had put too much makeup on her and she looked fake, her hair too curly and a forced smile drawn across her lips in a bright red shade that Mrs. Pickett would have never worn. She was swollen and squeezed inside the box, her arms pinched close beside her. One of the children, Mary Stella, an adopted one, the oldest, leaned over and kissed her dead mother on the lips and I remember thinking that the preacher better not make us all do that because I wasn't about to kiss a dead person. I touched her on the arm only because one of the boys dared me. It felt hard and stiff, tensed as if she were trying to make a muscle.

Miss Lucy curled herself up in a corner in the church fellowship hall. The social worker said that since she was retarded she couldn't understand that her sister had died; but I knew her balled up like that was the purest picture of grief I would ever see. She was tight, like a knot, trying to pull her arms and legs inside herself and disappear. I knew what she was doing because I had tangled myself up like that a few times too. It was grief all right. Miss Lucy knew.

Later, when the social worker came to take Miss Lucy to the state hospital, one of the foster children, May Anne, the young one, pulled a chair into the living room, stepped upon it, and took Mrs. Pickett's tiny doll with the silk black hair from the top shelf. She jumped down and placed it in Miss Lucy's hands.

Miss Lucy held the doll like a child holds her favorite toy, ruined because of someone's rough play, staring at it for what seemed a long time, and then she did what the social worker called an act of juvenile destruction. We, of course, Mrs. Pickett's wards and children, understood exactly what she was doing when she began pulling apart the little doll.

Quickly, deliberately, she yanked off its tiny arms and legs, even the head with the long silky hair, and gave each one of us five children a plastic body part, something of our own to have, something of her kindly sister.

After we were all moved to other houses, passed off to other families, I never again thought about death or even my life at Mrs. Pickett's. I never considered Miss Lucy and what she did on the day after her sister was put in the ground. Just sometimes when I took out that tiny pink doll arm and remembered how cold Mrs. Pickett felt when I touched her at the casket did I have long clear thoughts about dying.

Only a few times while I was growing up, alone and unattended, did I consider that once we are gone, we become like Miss Lucy's doll, pieces of our life torn and strewn about in the various places we have lived, in the pockets of those who knew us.

All of the days, I thought, that we are alive and breathing, we hold ourselves together in desperation. We keep our hands to ourselves, our fingers not too far-reaching, our hearts stilled behind chest walls. We dare not let our dreams fling us too distantly. We see only what lies in a restricted line of vision. But once we are dead, we are like a doll broken and dispersed to foster children; we are separated, divided, and will never be brought back together again. We are an unsolved puzzle with the pieces scattered and lost.

My life has been spent preventing all the parts of myself from exploding into fragments, keeping myself together, a lifetime of emotional management. But death was the permission to come undone, the slender plastic arm of a doll that I have kept with me like a charm.

I stayed with Olivia twenty minutes, maybe a little less, remembering that doll and Mrs. Pickett, and thinking about all the different ways a person can grieve. I thought about Miss Lucy, the preacher and a nurse trying to pull her out of that corner. I thought of Mary Stella running out of the church, screaming and refusing to be held. I remembered the other adopted child, Billy Mac, and how he threw rocks at his mother's bedroom window, leaving a crack that silently splintered into long, narrow lines.

I thought about the three foster children, how we all sat up straight in the hardback chairs, behaving ourselves, quiet, waiting to be told when to pack and where we'd be going next. Our grief was hard and cold, a stone hidden in our hearts. We had already faced our greatest losses and the only things we grieved any more were the little luxuries in which we had come to find pleasure. Mrs. Pickett's homemade cinnamon rolls, hot and buttery, the icing a glaze of sweetness. Soft terry-cloth towels or our own beds. New school supplies, a plastic lunch box. After a couple of years in the foster home program, a child carries few expectations, only memories of the one or two surprisingly delightful things we enjoyed in the other houses.

I straightened the gown Olivia was wearing and smoothed out the sheet across her chest, placing her arms down by her sides. I combed her hair and wiped her face with a cloth I found on the counter by the gurney. I even picked up the paper and trash from the floor around her bed and put it in the can near the door. I did everything I could think to do in the time I had alone with Olivia Jacobs except tell her good-bye. Since, in her leaving, she had never said a word of farewell to me, I realized in her death that I did not know how to say it to her. And since my grief was still locked in a box behind my heart, I did not know how or what I should feel.

I left the room and found Heather sitting at the nurses' station writing up a report. She seemed surprised when I approached her and she quickly glanced at the clock that hung on the wall just behind me. She smiled and came around the tall desk and handed me Olivia's belongings. They had been placed inside a white plastic hospital bag that was sitting just on the corner of the desk.

Inside the bag, she showed me, were Olivia's clothes and shoes, her watch, a tiny amethyst ring that she wore on her wedding finger, her glasses, and her purse with keys to a home I had never seen. The small piece of paper folded twice with my name and number had been carefully written and slipped in the zippered pocket on the outside of the purse. This note, Heather explained, was how they knew where to find me. The word "daughter," written under my number, was how they knew who I was.

I gave her the name of a local funeral home, chosen randomly from the yellow pages, said I couldn't yet think of a preacher, and I pulled the string at the top of the plastic bag and slung it across my shoulder.

Heather walked with me to the front desk of the emergency department and seemed disappointed that she hadn't been able to help me more with my grief. I smiled at her and held up a hand as the large glass doors opened and I moved near them. She waved back and I imagined that she would go home that night and tell her boyfriend or husband that a daughter came to see her dead mother that morning during her shift and hadn't even shed a tear.

She would tell it slowly and with a lot of sadness and discontent, troubled at how families no longer care for one another. Then later, after she had rinsed and placed the dishes in her new stainless-steel dishwasher, wrapped up the leftovers for her lunch the next day, and wiped the table clean, she would call her mother just to say hello, delighting her parents with her attentiveness and reminding them of how lucky they were to have such a dutiful daughter.

I got into my car and shut the door, yanking the seat belt around me. I waited while a truck pulled in beside me. A woman, the driver, got out, ran to the passenger's side, and opened the door. A man seated, his head wrapped in a bloody bandage, stood outside, and closed the door. He looked at me through my window, just for a second, and dipped his head, a polite greeting as the blood trickled down the side of his face, dripping beneath his right eyebrow, then turned to walk on to the emergency room. The woman, chasing him, waved her hands in the air, yelling at him to wait.

I stuck the keys in the ignition and then reached into the plastic bag that was sitting on my lap and took out Olivia's old black purse. I slid my fingers along the stiff leather handles. I fingered the zipper, pulling it back and forth, opening and closing it. I held it to my face and smelled it. Then I put it and the plastic bag on the passenger seat beside me, took out the set of keys from the inside compartment, and stuck them in my front pocket. I started the engine, and without really thinking about the decision I was making, began driving in a direction I had not planned, following the whim of a little girl I barely knew.

As I drove out of the parking lot I remembered one of Olivia's recent visits. It was about the sixth or seventh time she had come to our house, late in the evening, just around suppertime. It was like the other earlier visits. She called first, her voice quiet and yearning. She'd ask if it was appropriate if she joined us and I would answer yes. I would tell her what we were eating for supper and she would explain that she could wait until after we ate. I would remind her that there was always enough to share and she would mumble a word of thanks and be at my front door in less than thirty minutes.

She never ate much, "like a bird," I'd say to her; and she would nod and reply that she always got what she needed. She never talked much, just answered our questions, cautiously and thoughtful, like she knew what we were going to ask. Mostly, she just listened, fidgeted a lot and listened. To Anna who talked about her day at school, the homework, the struggles with the other girls, the way she longed for summer. Or to me, my complaints about work, the printer that was old and not working, the amount of paperwork in a college business office, the noise involved in the remodeling project in the building next to mine.

She was respectful, never offered advice or criticism, never stayed longer than a couple of hours, always helped me with the dishes.

On the visit I was remembering as I pulled away from the hospital, Anna asked her why she wouldn't let me drive her home. I had offered every time she got ready to leave, but she always politely refused, asking only that I call a number and tell the person who answered that Olivia was ready to go.

"Don't you want Mama to take you home?" my daughter asked, her brown eyes so full of innocence.

"My friend's a good driver," Olivia replied and left it at that.

I had not thought much about her refusals. I just assumed she liked her independence in coming and going or maybe even that she enjoyed spending time with the man who picked her up in his old brown Chevrolet, always waving in my direction before he backed away.

"Why's she so secretive about everything?" my daughter asked me one night after the thin dark man who drove Olivia to and from my house pulled out of the driveway. Anna waved good-bye to her grandmother and closed the front door.

"Maybe she just doesn't want me to drive her," I replied. I started drying the dinner dishes. Anna pulled the drapes closed and fell back against the sofa.

"Or it could be that she and her 'friend' got something going on." I grinned at her, raising my eyebrows as if I were giving juicy gossip, and watched as my daughter rolled her eyes.

There was a long pause before she spoke. She was watching a game show, the applause loud and ordered.

"Maybe she's ashamed of where she lives," she said thoughtfully. "Maybe she thinks that if you saw her house, you'd feel sorry for her and ask her to live with us."

I stopped drying and stacking and turned toward my ten-year-old child, amazed at her level of maturity, her perfectly detached insight.

Of course she was right. Olivia remained private about everything, about her reason for leaving me, the direction her life had taken, the place she called home, because she didn't want to elicit drama or pity from the daughter she abandoned. She shared nothing of who she was when she walked out of my life and who she was when she walked back in because it was just easier for me not to know.

If she lived in a spacious home with a guest room and a wide clean yard, then surely she knew I would wonder why she had waited so long to reunite. I would see that there was room for me and Anna to come and go and enjoy her smooth lace linens and thick sprawling gardens and I'd be angry that she hadn't shown up sooner. And if she lived in a shack, a rented room in a crack house on the edge of town where I had never ventured, I would certainly feel compelled to do something for her, provide her with a more comfortable arrangement.

I realized as I drove from the hospital heading in the direction of her recorded address that she was wise not to allow for either possibility. And as I moved toward where she lived, I understood she was more concerned about pity than she was about drama. She had not been living in a house of fine linens and full beautiful gardens. She did not have extra room for company. She had not been selfish with her things.

Long past rows of neatly groomed trees and flower boxes that lined blue and white shutters, I drove. Beyond the sidewalks and playgrounds that marked the good neighborhoods, I drove toward center of town where tall buildings and brows crossed in worry hide the sun. Beyond the pedestrian walkways and the women who hurry by in their uptown clothes and small sneakered feet, I turned down Lee Street and moved into an area of town that was unfamiliar and generally avoided by people who work so near its border.

I made the same circle twice, down beyond the boarded-up pool hall, out from Jimmy's Kash and Karry, and down around the back of a long brick building marked with a Community Hall sign, when I realized I was trapped inside a neighborhood that seemed to begin and end at the four-way stop in front of Calvary Hill Fellowship Baptist Church. Searching for the place where Olivia had stayed and only briefly mentioned was proving to be as much of a hardship as any other part of our journey. I was just about to turn around when I came to the street I knew to be the right one and quickly began to follow the house numbers.

Massey, the street where she lived, was off the hard-surfaced road on my left at the four-way stop, and was a short thoroughfare that dropped and curved until the pavement ended only a few hundred yards away from the intersection. The three hundred block consisted of only six duplexes close to the road on both the left and the right, all with white trim and cars lining the gravel drives. I inched ahead along the narrow passageway, past Margie's House of Beauty, and lines of clothes that waved and snapped, drying in the sun.

412 was a two-story old boardinghouse sided up next to a row of little white buildings and jutting out from the lawn like a broken tooth. There hanging from a tall rusted pole was a small green sign with the number 412 etched in gray paint and hardly legible in the shifting wind. Recently planted marigolds

circled the pole, adding a splash of yellow to the dusty, brown yard. An old tree, a sugarberry, stood just on the corner, just beyond the edge of the house, its limbs swinging low and the narrow leaves spinning in the breeze.

I parked on the street, in front of the tree, checking the locks on all four doors of the car. The area was quiet. Few vehicles passed and no one was outside that I could see. As I walked to the house I looked up the road, noticing how close the interstate was. Remembering the curves and the downtown traffic, I tried to determine if there was an easier exit than there had been entry, exercising another old foster home habit of mine.

This technique I had learned from a girl named Talitha. She was big for her age and stronger than anybody I had ever known. She had been in foster homes all of her life, dropped in a Dumpster at a hospital, just after she was born, and wrapped in a long brown potato sack.

She had gotten caught alone when she was five and gang-raped by some boys in an orphanage. She was in a coma for six weeks, having been beaten with a baseball bat. When she awoke, not having remembered exactly what had taken place, she was convinced that a bad thing had happened because she had gone down a hall and into a room that had just one door and a tiny window cut above the closet.

She remembered only that she had seen the small space above the closet opening, the glass pulled and locked, no room for even a little girl to slide through; and she had thought, just before she had blacked out, "This evil would not be happening if only I could fit through that window."

"Never go into a place you can't get out of," she instructed me when I was ten or eleven and had been punched and cornered by a girl four years older and forty pounds heavier. Talitha had pulled me out and away from her. She walked me into the family den, a room with long, open windows and two wide doors.

"Make sure there's another place you can run to, another room, or a window you can crawl through," she added as she checked my swollen lip to see if it was bleeding and then gently smoothed down my hair.

"A girl's gotta watch where she goes." And she held my quivering chin in her hand and nodded. "You'll learn," she said, smiling, " 'cause you're smart."

I have never called myself smart. I was only an average student in school, never won an award or got asked to go to college. But Talitha was right about part of what she saw in me. I did learn. I have always been careful about the rooms I would enter and stay.

I climbed four steps to a long porch that wrapped around the house and was empty except for two wooden rockers that moved with the motion of a slow, lazy thought. I knocked on the splintered screen door, wondering whom I might find inside and feeling the heat of the late morning sun as it slid down my neck. A few minutes passed when I heard the movement coming toward the door and was met by first a shadow and then a woman shaped like a child, not much bigger than Olivia.

Her hair was combed into rows of white braids that ended in frayed knots, circling her dark head like a crown of pearls. One of her eyes wandered away from the other as her right hand felt for the long, crooked lock on the door, making sure it was fitted into the small ring on the frame. She seemed as uneasy as I that I was standing on her porch.

"You here about Olivia Jacobs?"

I nodded.

The woman was chewing on the inside of her bottom lip, her forehead pressed into the meshed wire that separated us. "She dead, I guess." The old woman tilted her head, studying me with the one eye that didn't jerk. "You the daughter?" She asked like she had been waiting for me. "Alice," she added.

It surprised me to hear her say my name.

The late spring flurry was kicking up my dress and I fumbled with it to keep it down, aware of the presence of the empty rocking chairs that dipped and swayed more heavily.

"Yes," I answered softly.

The one eye gazed long before she pushed aside the lock and cracked the door. The wind pulled against the screen and wood; and I quickly stepped inside, the door closing hard behind me.

The old woman shuffled past a sitting room and turned to the stairwell saying nothing as I followed her, glancing from side to side to notice the pictures hanging on the wall. We walked up the steps, moving slowly toward the top and then again to the front of the house until she stopped at a brown-stained door with a cast-iron B nailed in the center.

"You got her key?" She was watching me now.

"Yes, it was in her purse." I reached inside my pocket and retrieved the small silver ring that bore the two keys, one marked with a red dot and one marked with a blue one, and handed them to the woman. She took the red key and slipped it into the lock, gently turning the knob.

"My brother's sold his farm east of town. City's putting a highway through it." The old woman handed me back the ring of keys. I could feel her studying me. "He's moving in here the first of the month." She slid her bottom lip from side to side. I wasn't sure why she was telling me this.

"You be out by then?" she asked, suddenly making herself clear.

I nodded slightly. "I should think so. I'm just here to get her stuff," I said, trying to focus on the woman's one good eye without looking curious or disrespectful.

She waited like she had something else to say and then turned without a reply, shuffling in the direction from which we had come, slowly moving down the stairs, leaving me alone in the place where Olivia had made her home.

It was a narrow room and cool. A single bed was pushed against one wall and a trunk was wedged between the footboard and the doorjamb. It was obvious that the space had been furnished by the house owner since the sparse furniture looked similar to what I saw in the sitting room when I entered and the walls were decorated with pictures not unlike those I passed on my way from the front door. Landscapes mostly, colorful prints of thick forests, cedars and firs, white oaks and silverbells, one of a cabin, deep in a grove of tall pines.

A large oval rug covered the center of the floor, adding cushion to my steps as I moved inside. A little cove in the middle of the wall to my left suggested a closet but was covered by a thin faded curtain, keeping its purpose a mystery. The room was dark and I searched for a light, finding a lamp on the table next to the door. I switched it on and then moved to the one window, pulling up the shade that hung low beneath the sill.

The light poured in, lifting dust and giving warmth to the darkness. I turned around to imagine what solace Olivia found here, to see what she saw the last days of her life. The single bed, the curtained cove, the pictures someone else had bought and hung, as sparse as it all seemed, there was still a sense of home. And yet, surely, my daughter was right. Even though the room and the house were fine, clean and safe, big windows and lots of exits, my mother must not have told us where she lived because she was ashamed.

There was a rocker placed near the window covered in heavy red velvet worn in the places where someone's haunches and neck, shoulders and back rested. It was turned toward the outside, facing the string of houses that pushed near the border of town leading to the interstate that stretched from east to west. I imagined that it was here that Olivia spent her time, remembering the past or planning some nearby future. It was here, I thought, where she decided to find me and gathered her courage to come to the other side of town.

I sat in the chair, trying to position myself in her prints. I tried to fit my shoulders where hers had rested, tried to lean into the back as she must have done. I pushed my legs down, the weight hard and firm where the cushion had given way like the earth when a path is made.

I pressed my head against the top of the chair, closed my eyes, and rocked. Back and forth. Back and forth. Moving toward and away from the window, toward and away from all that I knew, all that I remembered about a woman named Olivia Jacobs, a woman who had been my mother.

As I rocked, as I sat in that room that held Olivia's breath, her thoughts, her notions, as I fumbled through dreams and frozen scenes from my childhood, my mother laughing, the two of us spinning in sunlight, my mother holding me in her lap, I also rested. I was, perhaps, calmed by the motion, a child in the prints of her mother's arms, feeling the thing she felt, or maybe by the place, a house filled with strangers living so intimately, a long, cool room.

Or maybe it was because of the chair, borrowed and worn, the warmth of the sun against my face. Whatever it was that rested me also somehow fed my memories, nurtured what lay so quietly and hopefully near the surface of my heart. Her face, young and smooth, delighted, flashed before me; her hands, tender and soft, touching me. I found glimpses of her in my mind that I had imagined were gone.

I rocked for what seemed a long time and then I stopped. I opened my eyes, and following the path of the sun across the window, I noticed just to my right, just in the corner, a glimmering reflection from something in the room behind me. I stared at it, the small captured fleck of gold, and wondered of its origin, its content or nature. Then I turned to see the sun had caught the metal from the trim on Olivia's trunk. The buckle, shiny and unlatched, shimmered like a jewel in the morning light; and I stood and walked to it as if it had called my name.

I opened it carefully; and as if I knew what I would find, reached beneath a soft periwinkle sweater and skeins of blue and white yarn. I slid aside an old family Bible and some folders of bank statements. I pulled out and placed beside me a set of embroidered pillowcases and a pink electric blanket and found what had been hidden and treasured.

A dusty old scrapbook held together by a large rubber band had been slipped between clothes and covers, documents and handiwork. It was black, worn, and coming apart; but I knew it would tell me something. I knew it contained pieces of a story, elements of a life unspoken and unknown. I knew she had reason and purpose for each piece clipped and pasted to the thick faded pages. And as I opened this record of Olivia's story, this collection of poems and pictures, news articles and official letters, I knew she had saved them all for me.

I held the book to my chest, a frail and faded life, my heart beating loudly against it. I stood, walked back to the velvet chair, reclined in the familiar curves and prints, snapped off the rubber band, and began the journey of reading my mother's life.

Father of orphans and protector of widows
is God in his holy habitation.
God gives the desolate a home to live in.

—Psalm 68:6

One

1932 left North Carolina barren. Tobacco farms and cotton fields stood idle while farmers felt deep inside pockets of old pants and under mattresses and in between cushions, trying to find a nickel or maybe a dime that could mean shoes, sugar, or even seeds for the coming year.

Every spring it was a gamble. The prices. The boll weevil. The weather. And winter in the South was the outcome of casting the dice. This was the season of squeezing turnips and convincing each other that you were seeing blood. Of making something out of nothing. Like stretching a ball of dough into three meals and making a new dress with the seats and knees and seams from an old pair of trousers. From November to March there was nowhere else in the country where the men appeared so unsteady and the women so careful. And the southern farmer pushed through those months like a train slowing down before passing through a tunnel, trying to save a few pieces of coal.

Winter was the time for figuring. Long days and restless nights of deciphering survival as if it were a complex math equation with a simple solution that you can't find. Men trying to decide whether it was the mines of Appalachia or the factories up north that would lend them back the dignity that the farmland had stripped.

Women trying to make up rules and stories that would keep the children from getting lost in a dream that made them weak-spirited and unable to fight off diseases like tuberculosis and scurvy. Tenant farmers wondering how they can plant more tobacco in a row or which child will be old enough to join the others in the field. It was a low time and gray and folks went to bed trying to remember spring and the colors and the way they used to touch each other in the night.

North Carolina was lonesome for life. For some noise other than the shifting of prayers to get through the day or the busy silence that marked the beginning and ending of daily tasks. The whole state seemed to be folding up in old age. Land and river, field and meadow, every acre, every glance, seemed to be empty of any flower or seed. Except for the womb of Mattie Jacobs.

Here lay the faint movement of time that grew stronger each day, forming into heart and liver and breath-giving lungs. Brain stem pushing into spine and earthy brown eyes. Fingers grabbing and clutching. Legs curling and stretching. Each ticking of the clock signaling shape and span to the daughter who was dancing inside her. Mattie was going to give birth to one long, needful child.

The young woman had not planned to leave her home in

Mississippi, but circumstances prevented her from staying. She sensed a change in her body. She felt the stirring inside her, but she tried hard to make herself believe that it was only her restlessness and her need to get out of the Deep South.

Having heard of work and men in North Carolina, she packed up her few belongings, her five-year-old son trailing behind her, and headed north. By the time she crossed the state line she was late and she knew. But she still believed that she could make this baby go away just by denying it. It didn't work, but it didn't matter because even when the child was pushing through her clothes, she swore it was just a virus.

The young woman arrived in Greensboro, North Carolina, on a late day in March when winter was still bearing down. She got off of the bus, early in the afternoon, her son standing close behind her, and expected at the very least some man to greet her, carry her luggage, and help her find a place to stay. She was, instead, met with extreme disappointment when the only people she saw at the bus stop were three boys not much older than twelve who had a price set for every bag depending upon its weight and how far they had to walk.

"A penny for each one," the oldest of the three reported to Mattie when she asked how much it would cost for his help.

The young boys, impressed with the flash and style of the stranger whose dress clung in all the places they craved to touch, still charged her the same amount they had agreed upon for all who asked for their assistance. To save herself a few coins she made her little boy carry his own bag, needing the help of only one of her greeters.

"Well, darling," the young woman said to the boy who quoted her the price, "I reckon I'm just going to have to pay for your services." Then she laughed like what she said was sexy and smart, like she had suddenly become charming.

The boy blushed and picked up her bags, leading Mattie and her child in the direction of the boardinghouse just a few storefronts away.

The young woman paraded behind the boy slowly, her purse swinging easily at her side. Mattie was pretty. And she knew it. Tall and leggy, she always wore clothes that held tightly against her figure. She was proud of her curvy profile and often would stand to the side so that a man's eyes could appreciate the dips and turns her long line of body would take them.

She knew that without money and hardly any education that her figure was her only ticket out of poverty and loneliness. What she didn't know was how to distinguish between the sets of eyes that roamed across her wishing for a closer look. Her mama used to say she was so dumb she wouldn't know a man was bringing trouble if he stuck it in a marked box and carried it on his head.

She stood at the entryway of Barrett's Boardinghouse and paid the boy three cents. Then the crisp March wind blew open her coat. So she slid her hands just below her collarbones, outlining her breasts, down along her slim waist, and into the meeting of her thighs, then up again and across the bottom of her back, settling into the small of her spine. This, she decided, was his tip.

And with a wink and a smile from the mother of a too-silent child who stood watching, the boy who carried her bags stumbled over his feet and hurried away with a face as red as the new copper pennies that were buried deep into his palm. Pleased with herself, Mattie walked in the house, leaving her son alone on the porch.

She had not thought much about where she and Roy would live once they arrived in North Carolina. She had not thought much about anything except leaving. She had enough money to stay a few weeks at the boardinghouse, but she knew she was soon going to have to find a place that didn't charge by the night.

Miss Barrett pointed her to the farthest room upstairs and watched with a hint of worry as the woman in the tight dress walked shamelessly up the steps with the boy tugging tightly at her coat as it swung from her arm.

The old woman did not like children in her house and usually preferred middle-aged men as boarders, but two salesmen had already checked out and weren't returning to town for a month. She needed the money. So she gave the woman and her son a room but was relieved to find out it would only be for a couple of weeks.

Mattie was not prepared for city life. She had not considered a failed economy or the idea that she would not find a job. She had not realized that winter and the Depression had taken its hold on the cotton mill town and that opportunities for women were few and far between.

She tried Cane Mills and was told that the waiting list had a hundred names on it though she was welcome to add hers to it. She hitched a ride to High Point to Amazon Mill where the women worked side by side with their children and lived in a company community with white frame houses and indoor toilets.

"All positions are filled," read the note on the front door. She rode over to the hosiery mill and stood in line to talk to a big red-faced man who stared at her breasts and licked his top lip but offered her no employment. She walked to two furniture factories and even took the bus to Winston-Salem, seeking a career of rolling tobacco shavings and packing them into paper. The news was the same. Nothing was available.

It was Claude Smithson who finally got Mattie work. His sister-in-law's cousin ran a beauty shop near the edge of town and she was trying to find someone to help her sweep up the place, clean the sinks, and do occasional manicures.

Claude had noticed the dark-haired beauty when she gave Reevie Daniel his tip on the day she arrived. Since then, he made a point of hanging around the old boardinghouse to offer himself as a driver or a baby-sitter just so he could watch the way she slid her hands across herself, the curves and the bends outlined by her fingers.

"I think you'll like Kay Martha," Claude told Mattie as he drove her to the shop. "And I think she mentioned that she may even have a place for you and your boy to stay." He smiled, sure that getting her a job and a house would have to mean something to the young woman who had caught his eye.

Mattie turned to her driver. Her skin itched from the wool sweater she was wearing. "Then I guess you think I owe you now."

He focused on the road, embarrassed that she had read his thoughts. She moved closer to him, rubbing her leg against his.

"It's all right, Claude. A party will do us both good." And she leaned up and blew lightly in his ear.

Claude pulled away from her and glanced in the rearview mirror. The little boy was asleep on the backseat and the man was relieved. He was uncomfortable with how Mattie never seemed to care what she said or how she acted in front of the child.

When they pulled up to the shop she jumped out quickly. "Just come get me this afternoon," she told him, "and make sure Roy doesn't sleep all day."

Then she headed inside Kay Martha's House of Good Looks, confident that the job was already hers.

The owner was cleaning up the bottles of shampoo and conditioner when Mattie walked in.

"I'm Mattie Jacobs," she said and stuck out her hand. "I'm here about the position."

Kay Martha walked around the table and took the young woman's hand. Claude had said she was pretty and outgoing, and the salon owner was immediately impressed.

"I'm Kay Martha," she responded. "Here, have a seat." She was heavyset, middle-aged, a pleasant woman who had a good head for business.

"So, Claude tells me that you just moved here." She sat down across from her.

"Yes, mam," Mattie answered, "from Mississippi."

"Oh, please," Kay Martha responded, "none of that polite stuff here, okay?"

Mattie nodded.

"And Claude says you have a son?" Kay Martha searched out the window for the child.

"Yeah, but he ain't any trouble," Mattie answered. "Claude watches him a lot. He really ain't much trouble," Mattie repeated.

"Yes, I'm sure he isn't," the woman replied.

They talked about the weather and the coming spring and the shop; and they discovered that Claude had been right. They did like each other. Kay Martha was sure that the presence of such a young and attractive woman would bring in customers. And she enjoyed Mattie's slow way of talking, her pleasing personality.

Mattie was happy to be with a woman who didn't seem concerned that she had on too much makeup or appeared worried that she might steal a husband; and she could tell that the older woman was easy to be with, uncomplicated.

"Well," Kay Martha began, "the job is basically just cleaning up, maybe a few manicures if we can get them. Mostly, I need an assistant; but if you like the job and want to learn more, I'm happy to teach." She nodded toward a couple of certificates taped to the wall. "I finished first in my class at beauty school."

"I'm happy to do whatever you need," Mattie responded. "I

am very good with a nail brush. I do my own nails." And she threw out her hands for inspection.

Kay Martha held Mattie's hands in hers and noticed how carefully the polish had been applied. She approved.

"I think you'd be great." And she patted the top of Mattie's hand. "The job is yours if you'd like it."

Mattie yanked the woman into her arms in a hug. "Thank you so much! I will work very hard," she promised, "starting now."

Kay Martha pulled away, surprised. "Well," she said, smoothing down the front of her dress. She glanced around the salon. "Okay, empty the trash first, if you don't mind," she told Mattie, watching as the young woman rolled up the sleeves of her sweater, "and then we'll wash out the combs and brushes."

Mattie did everything she was instructed. Later that morning she mixed up a perm solution and learned how to make appointments and keep up with receipts. She discovered how to fold the towels and where to keep the broom and dustpan. Then she finished the day once again showing off her steadiness with nail polish, giving Kay Martha a manicure with a color of Pretty in Pink.

When Claude returned to pick Mattie up, both of the women wore bright polish on their fingernails and lots of curls in their hair. They were chatting like old friends. The job and a place to stay, just at the end of town, were hers.

Kay Martha first mentioned the house to Mattie while they ate lunch together. She fixed them plates of navy beans and white bread and explained that the old place wasn't much. "Just a small cabin, really," she said. "It was the house where my grandfather lived a long time ago."

Empty for years and starting to fall down, she confessed. However, she told Mattie that she didn't care about deposits or contracts, that she just wanted someone to work on it, live in it, keep it from rotting on the foundation.

Kay Martha knew that Claude was a carpenter and seemed to have an interest in the new woman in town; so she thought he wouldn't mind patching the holes and putting in the new flooring. She thought it was a good arrangement for everybody. She'd get the place in working order and would not have to pay a penny. And the young mother and her little boy from Mississippi would have a home for just the two of them.

Later when he heard about the house, where it was and what was needed, Claude reluctantly agreed to fix it. He wasn't happy about the new living arrangements for Mattie and Roy because he thought it was not a good location for a woman and child. He thought it was dangerous and unsuitable since it was out of Greensboro and just on the edge of what most folks referred to as Smoketown.

The little shack, he found out, was right off the main road, down and across the street from the Pinetops Baptist Church; and as far as what the rest of the town saw, it was the beginning or ending of life depending upon what direction you were starting from. Smoketown was not a place, in the minds of lots of people, including Claude, that anyone should call home.

Everyone knew that it was the last house that church ladies

visited to invite folks to worship, the final stop for the white salesman who carried silk stockings and new cleaning supplies in a suitcase that hung low at his side; and it was the turn-around mark for children riding bicycles.

However, despite Claude's reservations and the shocked reactions of some of the other residents in Greensboro, Mattie seemed unconcerned about the location of her new dwelling and was just glad to get away from the boardinghouse where visitors were not allowed after dark.

The landlady was as rigid and stifling as Mattie's memory of Mississippi. So it didn't matter to her if all the white people raised their eyebrows and sucked their teeth when she told them where she lived, she just wanted something that was all her own. And even though none of the women who came into the beauty shop could believe it, Mattie actually liked the place. It was an adequate house for a mother and child, roomy, with walls thick enough for privacy and thin enough not to close her in.

"Room to breathe," she would say to Kay Martha, "and space to play."

Kay Martha thought, of course, that she meant for Roy, her little boy. But Mattie hardly ever thought of anyone but Mattie. The play space was meant for herself.

Regardless, however, of his mother's desires and intentions, Roy liked their new home too. He was given his own room next to the door leading to the kitchen with a window that leaned out to the side where his neighbors lived. The glass was broken in several places; and especially late on Sunday afternoons, he could smell the food cooking next door and hear the low hum of people laughing. He didn't have a bed, but Kay Martha had given them plenty of quilts so he had a pallet that was soft and drowned out the noises from where his mother slept and entertained company.

Just after they moved in, Claude painted the walls in the boy's room blue, like the sky, and Roy fell asleep every night feeling as if he were resting on a cloud, completely alone and free. The child thought this was the best he had ever known. The best house. The best bed. The best walls. The best neighbors. The best window. And it would be to these days that the young boy as a grown man would crawl back to and remember as the very best that life had ever offered him. Since there wasn't much good to consider before the move to Greensboro, the house on the edge of Smoketown was the only kind place he could recall.

Roy's birth was completely unexpected for Mattie. Before he was born she had never known the possibility of motherhood and had not considered the consequences on the afternoon that he was conceived. That too had come as a total surprise.

Mattie had met Roy Sr. at a Christmas party that her church gave at the local Children's Home. It was the preacher's idea as a way to teach the children in Sunday School about missions.

Mattie, never really interested in church activities, went with the other young people because it kept her from having to clean the outhouse or gather eggs at home; and it kept her away from her father, who was known to swing a belt as often and as hard as he swung the ax to cut wood for the stove, which at the Jacobs house was always burning.

Roy Sr. was an orphan. He and Mattie noticed each other while the Sunday School teacher and the other youth gave out the presents. There were bags with an orange, an apple, some nuts, and a stick of peppermint. She handed him his bag, beaming as she held it out; but he would not take it and rather glanced around at the other children, rolled his eyes, and walked out the front door.

She followed him as he moved away, the rest of the group singing carols and reciting Bible verses, calling out behind him, "Orphan boy, here's your bag. Don't you want your candy?"

She followed him because of the longing that stirred beneath the clear blue of his eyes. She followed him because she was curious about a poor orphaned boy who would not take her gift, a homeless boy who lived in a dormitory. She followed him because she could not understand why he had rejected what she knew to be the Christmas wish of every orphan child. She followed him, down the hall, to the screen door, out past the dirt field where the children's games were played, and into the edge of the forest.

The way the boy moved in and out of the trees, slow and provoked, made Mattie think of the story she had heard about a tiger in a traveling circus. The tiger had escaped, terror unleashed, and headed up along the river toward Arkansas, ravenous and feral. It had been shot four times before it fell; but no one had ever been able to find the dead or wounded body.

The boy seemed as angry and wild and as loose as the beast that had killed its trainer before stretching itself in madness toward the woods. And Mattie understood the blue-eyed boy as she would the runaway tiger, certain of the danger and desire. In spite of what she knew, she lay as calm as the sleeping baby Jesus when she pulled up her dress and offered herself as if she were the African jungles, the green and gold pastures that she considered to be the dream of every circus animal.

There were no words spoken between them. When he quivered inside her for the last time, he just got up, pulled up his pants, picked up the bag of fruit that lay at her side, handed her the stick of peppermint, and walked away. And Mattie just lay there thinking about the price of freedom, wondering if the circus trainer and the tiger spoke before one was mangled and one ran off.

She knew Roy's name because she had seen it stenciled on the inside of his collar as he lay on top of her. The letters were in dark brown and she had watched as they moved from his shirt and disappeared into his skin. A name stamped on his clothes like a prisoner's number. His only form of identity. ROY in big brown letters that slid off of the material and clung to his neck.

Although her daddy beat her until she fainted, she never told who the father was. And even up until the very hour that they left Red Banks, Mississippi, six years later, people were still whispering about whose child it was.

By the time he was born, Mattie couldn't remember what

Roy looked like so she wasn't sure if the baby resembled his father or not. He had her hair, dark and stringy, but his skin color was not like her olive complexion but more yellow. Not jaundiced really, just pale and slight.

He was born with a thin red line that wrapped around his neck that was a constant source for curious stares and Judas talk. Before he was delivered the umbilical cord had gotten tangled, cutting off his air supply. When he came out his face was all bruised, tinged, and cloudy. The midwife, worried that he might be dead, quickly unwrapped the cord and popped him on his butt. The baby immediately coughed and cried, seeming as normal as any other child except for the small bloodred ring that circled around his neck.

He had blue eyes. These Mattie knew came from his father since hers were as dark as mud. They had the same longing in them too, a wildness, a hint of sorrow, that she remembered from the orphan and the stories of the circus tiger.

The child was hardly a bother to his mother. It was almost as if he knew right from the beginning that he was a surprise and that for Mattie, surprises rarely entertained her. He was therefore glad to have the attention of his mother's employer, Kay Martha. He was happy to go with Mattie every day and stay in the salon. He liked the way Kay Martha spoke softly to him or slipped him a piece of licorice candy or sang him a silly song to ease him into sleep. He liked her stories about all the women who sat in the big chairs and how she almost married each and every one of their husbands but how something always happened to prevent her nuptials.

The child and the woman would listen to the complaints about their husbands' dirty feet and loud poker games and Kay Martha would suddenly hear the emptiness rising in her own heart. She would smile, showing just the right amount of empathy; and then when they would leave she would turn to Roy, staring into those sad blue eyes, and say, "Certainly don't have those problems here, do we, Roy?"

And with that coming after her last appointment, the shop would fall as silent as the little boy-child. Kay Martha would sigh, giving the day over, glad for the company of Roy and his mother who was outside washing towels.

Mattie had no problem with the new relationship her son had formed with her boss. She was glad that someone cared for the boy since she knew that she only had very little to offer her firstborn. There just never seemed to be room in her life for a child choking from birth.

It just wasn't in her to be a mother. And she could not manufacture what everyone thought should come naturally. This lack of maternal instincts however was only part of the reason she pretended that the widening of her belly was only about her and not about another child. The event of that conception was not so much a surprise as it was a tragedy; and even though a number of months had separated her from the sorrow, she was still trying hard to forget. She left Mississippi, confident that the move would ease the memories; and she was hopeful that her new home would brighten her future.

Mattie's new place at Smoketown was next door to two women and two small children whose house seemed to be a favorite gathering spot for the people who lived farther up the road. It was a bright dwelling with a thick, ripe vegetable garden in back and tall, sturdy hollyhocks and black-eyed Susans strung around the steps and all along the borders. Spring decorated the driveway and danced out into the street at Mattie's neighbors' house.

There was color everywhere, in the trees, on the path, in window boxes, on the kitchen table; and it was soon understood by Mattie and her little boy what everyone else already knew, that this was a place of pure sweetness.

Ruth was known for her cooking skills and the delight of her company; and the smells of catfish frying or a rabbit stewing, pinto beans boiling and cornbread popping, drifted from her kitchen like a signal to the rest of the community. A signal that welcomed hungry spirits and starved appetites for something wonderful. A signal that softened the heat of the summer and wiped the edge away from a cruel winter. A signal that promised the taste of something sugary or filling, a signal that led them to a place in their souls that gathered all the joyful things in life and held them there waiting to be remembered.

Some thought it was Ruth's choices of seasonings, bay leaf and salted pork in stews and greens, cinnamon and just a pinch of ground nutmeg in her pies, rosemary in her soups, that made grown men forget about the ache in their hands from the longing of muscles to work and feel instead the desire of their youth that teased and pulled at their crotches.

Others imagined that it was Ruth's use of dairy, cream for the peaches and blueberries, butter on top of jams instead of beneath them, milk in the cornbread, that allowed women to loosen the tight reins of privation that kept their heads bowed and shoulders squared and made them want to open their legs and feel the breeze that tickled their softness and curved inside them like a wish.

Everyone understood that there was something about Ruth's grandness in creating dishes, her kind and ample heart, and all that color around her house that could make the folks in Smoketown forget the darkness of their skin and how they would curse themselves and, worse, each other.

Ruth's house was like a poultice and it dried the soreness and eased the weightiness of a pain that was so old it did not need a name.

She had two children. A boy only two days older than Roy and a baby girl who still only knew life to be as ready and as supple as her mother's nipple. The boy was named Edward Saul after a great-uncle who was shot four hours after a Union officer came onto the plantation and read the Emancipation Proclamation. It was told that after the officer left, the white man lined his slaves up and shot them all, men, women, and even the children, including three-year-old Edward Saul, whose last words to his mama were, "We free."

Miss Nellie was Ruth's mother and she had asked her daughter to move in with her eight days after her wedding to Ticker. She realized the trouble her son-in-law would be and believed that she would be called upon to protect what her daughter could not.

She was the one who had given Edward Saul the nickname

E. Saul because two syllables were easier than three and cleaner than one. She had already noticed how the little boy played with words like they were building blocks; and Miss Nellie was the one who knew that this child was meant to be more than a farmhand or some white man's boy. Miss Nellie could tell. Like a secret gift she had, she could tell. And she knew she would hang on to any thread of life just to see her dream unfold in her grandson.

The baby's name was Teresa but they called her Tree because her eyes were as steady as wood and her skin was as smooth as hickory bark. She was healthy and strong, born easy and without much pain to Ruth; and she slept in the arms of anyone because that was just the kind of child she was. Even Mattie asked to hold the little girl who could crinkle her face into a knot, then yawn back into sleep.

The first time, in fact, that Mattie spoke about the child she was carrying and ignoring was when she held Tree. "I wonder if this child is a girl," she had said with only a slight interest.

"I believe it is, Mattie, since you carrying it so high." Ruth smiled, remembering how Tree practically rested under her ribs. "Trying to get near her mother's heart," she told people.

She had realized before anybody else that Mattie was pregnant and pretending not to be. She had recognized the clear complexion and the blue look in the mornings even before Kay Martha. She mentioned it to Miss Nellie but chose not to say anything to her neighbor because she could see that Mattie was not acting like a woman about to give birth.

Ruth felt a deep sense of relief then when Mattie finally acknowledged what she had known for months. And she thought the acknowledgment was the start of her neighbor's acceptance of her pregnancy; but that simple statement did nothing to change Mattie. Because even though the denial loosened and made room inside her spirit, there was nothing new to fill its place. The hunger still pushed deep and tight, heavier than the opening body that grew inside her.

She could not stop herself from going across town to Percy's Pool Hall or Tiny Clayton's juke joint down near Buffalo Creek. Not even the polite proposal of marriage from Claude Simpson could ease what made her jumpy or give up what kept her steady. And over time she continued to return home from those places with some broken-down fool who didn't care or didn't see that the woman he was screwing was enough months pregnant to bring the presence of another set of eyes watching. She figured if a baby was coming it would just have to come; but as always, it would be her choice whether or not to spread her legs.

Mattie grew bigger and bigger, but so did her denial and her resistance to motherhood. Even in a new state, with a new job, and her own house surrounded in sweetness, her appetite for something she could not name could never be filled.

Then finally, when autumn fell behind the earth, the baby dropped, the color from next door faded, and her new house, the place she called home, the place that sat just at the edge of Smoketown, breathed and made room for the one she could not.

What makes one patch of ground fertile?
another dry as dust?
Who blows the breeze across a plant?
Who trims a pond in crust?
A dream is memory's bastard child
who quietly starts to die
and smothered by a mother's eye
hushed in silence lies.

—ES

Two

The month of November roared into the southeast with a storm that folks marked memories by. There were high winds and low dark clouds that opened up and rained down large rocks of ice, denting tractors and rooftops of buildings. Hail the size of baseballs broke the necks of chickens and hammered deep into the backs of cows and horses. It was a storm that started with ice and ended with a frozen rain leaving lungs damp and aged joints inflamed.

Pneumonia and an influenza virus began haphazardly wiping out the very young and the very old. The expected misery of winter began with a long wail of death that keened from General Lee Water's farm at one end of town to the far edge of Smoketown where some gypsies lived in tents.

Mattie was at home taking a nap when the baby started to drop. The young woman had been inside all week because of the storm and the advanced stages of her pregnancy, unable to get out because of the weather and her swollen ankles and dizziness from hypertension.

Ruth had come knocking on Roy's window on the day before the birth and motioned him around front, where she delivered some biscuits and sorghum molasses. She sprinkled ashes across the steps and all along the porch; and when she got to the sitting-room window she caught a glimpse of Mattie and she knew her time was near.

The first pain that hit Mattie caused her to scream so loudly that Ruth heard it over icicles breaking and falling from the tops of trees and the edges of gutters. It was louder than Tincan's rooster that crowed every time the sun peeked from behind a cloud, fooling itself into believing a new dawn had come. And it was even heard above the groaning and the tearing hearts of folks that gathered in Ruth's front room and along the hallway and into the kitchen.

The people from Smoketown had just returned from a funeral and they were trying to sort through an evil. An evil so big and so frightening that they knew they had to make it smaller or it could never fit into their minds.

Three days before the storm silenced the land and covered the earth in a blinding plague of ice and hail, the white preacher at Pinetops had cut down the limp and lifeless body of Elton Williams that swung from the big oak that stood way in the back near the cemetery.

Elton had last been seen playing basketball over at the park where the white boys assembled to smoke cigarettes and hide out from fathers and teachers and anyone else who did not believe in idle time. Calvin Hiatt and Sodapop Lody had tried to make him leave when the Johnson brothers drove up, but Elton had said it was their court too.

Calvin and Sodapop left just as three blond skinny boys spit out their toothpicks and rubbed their hands together with a grin like they were glad to see a black person. Elton turned, catching a final glance of the hind parts of his friends running through a grove of trees, then turned back, and with a look of defiance shot the ball from half court.

Later when they would walk up to the coffin and touch the swollen eye sockets or wonder to themselves if he was wearing shoes, Sodapop and Calvin would still hear the sound of the ball first against the flat piece of pine that served as the backboard and then the rolling in the peach basket before it fell through. Elton had yelled out something but neither boy could recall what it had been, remembering only the thud and spin that used to be the noise of winning.

The service had been postponed and rescheduled three times because of the storm; but even with the late date, the ice and the snow, as well as the old fear and the recent grief, were still just as heavy as they were the day Elton had been laid out in the front room of his grandfather's house.

All of Smoketown gathered at the church, mothers clutching to their children, men fidgeting in their pockets. The preacher spoke of heaven and a final resting place, but the people could only wrestle with the question of whose boy was next. The choir sang and the family read the cards of sympathy and condolence, but nobody saw this funeral as a celebration of a homecoming. A child of their own had been hunted down and killed and even though religion was the only salve they had to rub on the festered places in their spirits, it was not enough. It was never enough.

They left the church and gathered at Ruth's house, the way they always did after festivity or disappointment. The food was hot and plenty, but no belly was filled with delight or satisfaction on this occasion.

Ruth and Miss Nellie passed around bowls of canned beans and plates with pieces of fried pork, but the dishes just came back, still warm and full. They walked around with pitchers of iced tea and a pot of coffee, but no one seemed to want any food or drink. Everyone stood around, silent and empty.

Even with the windows closed and the doors shut, it wasn't hard to hear the scream of Ruth's next-door neighbor. She was resting and unprepared; so that when she felt that first contraction of labor, a full minute of searing, perfect pain, she yelled with a force that pushed her from the bed.

"Lord, it's that girl for sure; the baby is coming! I'm going to need some help." Ruth put down a pan of salted rinds and went to her bedroom to get her coat.

Earlene Petite stopped rocking. Reverend Irvine quit picking at his teeth and saying, "Dear Jesus." Even Masie Williams ceased shaking her head from side to side, glancing up in disbelief. The house grew as quiet as Miss Nellie ever knew it could be. The air was heavy and sad; and they swallowed, aware of the thickness of their tongues and the dryness at the back of their throats.

Everyone stared at the ceiling or at their feet and still nothing moved.

"Well," Ruth said as she returned to the room, pulling her arms through her coat, "ain't nobody gonna help?"

Miss Nellie glanced up, trying to get a better picture of her daughter with an attempt to understand where such a pristine force as her love could have been born and grown. She knew that Ruth never thought about how much she gave away. She never realized who got her last piece of sweetbread or the first taste of stew. She never questioned if something from around the house was missing or when somebody was going to pay her back if they stopped off to borrow thirty cents before going into town. Her mind always seemed to be on higher things and it was that spirit of complete unselfishness that brought these mourners there in the first place.

Most everyone knew of the only time when Ruth was less than charitable and since they were partly responsible they could not hold that against her, not that they ever would anyway. That deed was justified and buried and never resurrected for discussion or afterthought. She was a woman with a soul as gentle as dusk. And that's why no one could look her in the eye when she starting making steps toward delivering the white woman's child.

It was Josiah Smith who finally spoke and it surprised everyone in the house that he was the one to name it. Having always and only been a man of quiet suffering, he had been the picture of submission.

Josiah never fought or ran off when the white man tore up

the deed to his father's land, causing his family to lose the only thing sharecroppers ever really dreamed of. He didn't make threats about how he was going to get revenge like his brother did before he had disappeared late one Christmas night. He didn't protest when his nephew was arrested and whipped after a white woman said he winked at her while walking down the street and he didn't flinch when the police picked him up because he looked like a man who had stolen chickens from a farmer in town.

He had borne his injustices like a man who understood to fight would be to lose. He had kept silence like it was a vow, managed humility like he was studying to be one of Christ's chosen disciples. He had been beaten down, lied to, laughed at, and stolen from; and he had never demonstrated a flicker of anger or resentment.

But something had happened in this storm. Something deep and far inside him had weakened and cracked. Like the tops of the pines that lay strewn all around them, split and fallen, he was broken by what had happened to a teenage boy who had only wanted to play ball. And he was finally unable to hold his tongue while his neighbor and friend was planning to dole out charity and goodwill on a day of such sorrow.

He cleared his throat and spoke with a strong but stretched voice. The others turned to him, curious and disbelieving. "Miss Ruth, you gonna go and bring another white child in this world when ours being killed out?"

It was an innocent question and simple; but he did not lift his eyes nor did he feel the room as it swayed and then steadied.

He did not see the uneasy pats of hands on legs or the shaking of so many heads.

Ruth stopped and turned to the question, to Josiah, and the people of Smoketown gathered in her house. She was suddenly aware of the air's heaviness and the consequences of evil. There had just been a lynching, a boy kidnapped and murdered; and everyone, including the kind and gentle Ruth, knew that justice would never be served.

She went around the room peering into the faces that told the stories of all the painful memories that each soul bore. The "yes, mams" and the "no, sirs" that held them down under the iron hand of oppression. The simple truths about where they could and could not go for dry goods or use the toilet or even ask a question. The envy that ate away at the bottom of their hearts for those who walked within a lighter shade and could pass into a world that all the others only watched from a distance. The wide-eyed fear of a mother when a son doesn't come home from an afternoon of playing with his friends.

When she reached Masie Williams's face, she had to turn away and close her eyes, the mother's sorrow so new and so tightly bound. Then she took off her coat and walked over to the woman who used to clap her hands together when she laughed, always saying, "Mercy!" as if the laughter was going to kill her.

Now the laughing woman was hollow. And Ruth knew that she would never again call out for mercy because she could not understand what it could possibly do for her now.

"Mrs. Williams, what happened to your baby was wrong, as

evil as the world can get, and I know your heart is splitting. I know you can't see how you gonna move through tomorrow with your son's blood smeared across your mind." She knelt down in front of the dead boy's mother, her knees tired from years of praying and scrubbing, her joints aching from the cold.

"But, Mrs. Williams." Ruth took a breath and swallowed hard. She steadied herself on the principle of grace.

"One dead child is no good reason for two." And with that and one long and deep pause of sympathy she gave to everyone, she eased herself up from the floor and walked to the door, leaving a house empty of pardon and full of grief.

It was bad. Not only the labor but also the confused presence of a five-year-old whose soul had been throttled. Not only the lack of supplies and assistance but worse was Mattie's decision not to allow the baby to be born. As far as she was concerned, this whole thing was a mistake and she just wanted the error erased and her life to return to the way it was before the storm.

She screamed out for a drink because she was tired of flesh tearing and the push from deep inside her. She was tired of the needle-sharp ice and the rain that battered her sleep. She was weary from the howling wind that ripped around the corners and snuck in beneath doors and across sills of windows. She was spent from the weight of her belly and the story that washed across her dreams of how it came to happen.

This conception was not like Roy's. The baby, this life, transpired over months of Mattie's short youth. Months of the first love that Mattie Jacobs had ever known; and because of the hungry scars it left, it would be the last. And as she fought the delivery, trying hard to forget, the memories rained down.

Paul Wade was just passing through Red Banks, Mississippi, when he first laid eyes on Mattie. She was walking on the side of the road, her sandals tied and swinging from her shoulder. Her dress, damp, catching in between her legs while she sauntered through the tall grass, stopping to pick up stones and pitch them to the wind. Paul had hitchhiked up from Panola County where he was running from bad debts to folks you only owe once. And although he was in a hurry to get out of the state, he stopped the driver and jumped from the back of the truck trying to catch up with the young beauty who tossed rocks like a boy.

Paul Wade was quite the charmer and he folded Mattie up and slid her in his breast pocket before they ever got to Walker's Mill, just a mile from her daddy's farm. She, of course, did some folding of her own; and the bends of her smile left him shortsighted and weak-minded and he soon forgot that he was running.

It seemed only natural after their meeting that they would set up house together. And they moved to a shack up near the dip in Arkabutla River and decided to be born all over again. Mattie left Roy with her parents, trying to forget how hard her father could swing a belt, thinking that maybe since he was a boy, it wouldn't hurt or maybe her father wouldn't hate him as much.

She went to the river pretending not to have noticed that a black cat darted across her path just moments before that truck passed her and backed up, pretending not to have seen how Crazy Etta eyeballed her in town, lacing her fingers in and out of each other like she was delivering the makings of a curse. She went to the river for a little piece of happiness and she pretended not to have remembered anything before this man from Panola County followed her home.

And the river was sweet water and clear. And the days were easy and long. The nights cool and hushed. And they thought of nothing except where her back curved and the saltiness of his skin, the loose way he laughed and the rose of her cheeks. That was enough to fill each other's dreams and steal away any other memories.

Roy never asked about his mother. He assumed she was gone for good and it did not make him sad. He bore the brunt of her punishment and he never wished for anything except maybe wings and a tiny bit of sky. He was surprised when she came back, but it did not cause him any change of emotion or shift in feelings toward her. Instead, he only noticed the difference in her that was marked by twigs twisted and caught in her hair and a blank space in her eyes where he used to see light.

Mattie was down past the river in a hot spring when she heard the shot and felt the icy finger run along her spine. She hurried to get out of the water, but she got tangled in some branches that hung low near where she bathed. She called out Paul's name, hearing only the panicked kicking of the water and the ripping of her hair as she fought to get free.

After some time she finally grew tired from the struggle and hung from the tree in defeat. She looked up and saw a tongue gliding over lips and a wisp of smoke that drifted from the barrels of a gun pointed at her head. A man watched, enjoying the scene beneath him, aroused as the naked Mattie battled with a river tree.

She focused on the dark holes aimed at her eyes as she dangled like a fish caught on a hook. Another shot rang from the shore and Mattie saw the barrels lower as the bullet hit right above her head breaking apart the branches and dropping her into the warm water. The weight of the limb pushed her deep beneath the surface and when she came up, the thought of fighting and the gunman were gone.

Mattie found and picked up pieces of her lover that had been blown away in the blast. Along with arms and legs and a shattered face, there were tiny scraps of clothing and slender patches of skin. There was muscle, tight and spongy, and puddles of blood that she tried to lift from the dirt and hold in her arms. She picked up shards of glass and small smooth stones and could not decide which parts came from him and which parts did not. Without knowing for sure she piled them all together and placed them in the rowboat they had used for fishing.

She unstopped the hole in the bottom, pushed the boat offshore, and watched as all the pieces she could and could not name as being Paul Wade, all the things he was and was not, floated to the middle of the river and went down.

When she arrived at her father's house she did not smell of river water, nor did she give the appearance of a woman who had ever bathed in tenderness. She simply headed to her bedroom, grabbed some of her belongings, and headed north, feeling a stirring inside her that she was sure would drown or at least evaporate with time. Her five-year-old son ran behind her, catching up with her before she could send him back home.

"Mattie, you got to help! Push girl, push!" Ruth was all sweat and worry; her arms pressed between closed thighs, her fingers trying to find a passageway.

Mattie felt herself begin to fall into the arms of a gnarled river tree that wrapped around her waist and began to pull her down. She struggled to keep the knotty hands from forcing her into the water and she fought the thorny branches that tangled around her, holding her back from reaching the shore. She shoved forward and felt a thrust come from the smooth muscles that lined her womb as she watched the water mark rise.

"Mattie, you hear me? Mattie, girl, hold open your eyes, look at me! LOOK AT ME!"

Mattie opened her eyes and saw the frantic face of her neighbor, but just above Ruth's head she saw the silver barrels of a shotgun, a darting tongue, and a trail of smoke. She felt the smooth muscles tighten and the limbs snap behind her neck.

"O Lord, Mattie, O live, child, Lord, let this child live." Ruth was chanting and praying and trying to find a way to pull at the crown of the baby's head that was just beginning to show.

Mattie saw the spinning bullet as it left the barrel followed by a small blue flame. She felt the kicking and the squirming of her feet and arms and something else as she tried to break free from the twisted bough. She lifted her spine and gave out one loud and powerful yell that for her was the pain of a bullet flying through flesh and for Ruth was the energy behind just enough of a push to allow her to reach her hands in and grab on to a bloody, fighting baby.

Finally she curved her fingers around the tiny head and yanked the baby out. Ruth backed away from the bed and fell against the wall, the child stretched and struggling in her arms. "Mattie Jacobs, it's a girl. One fine messy girl!"

Ruth hurried to clean out the baby's mouth and waited for the pitch of a newborn's lungs. The infant squirmed and flinched and wrinkled up her face and then finally squalled out her existence. Ruth laughed in the pleasure of her success and laid the baby on Mattie's belly.

Mattie opened herself up when the bullet passed through her and she saw the face of Paul Wade as he leaned across her and blew a kiss. She glanced up expecting to see the smile of her lover and instead saw the head of a little girl with blood smeared along her cheeks.

"I believe this one is more stubborn than you, Mattie. I expect she'll need a strong name for such a fight as this." Ruth was standing between Mattie's legs cleaning up the afterbirth.

It was a long time before the new mother spoke. Ruth cleaned up the mess on the bed and on the floor, washing off the blood and mucus that had spilled all around them. She wrapped the baby in a clean towel and was looking out the window, watching as her friends and neighbors were leaving her house, when Mattie finally called out.

"You named her, Ruth." The woman, spent and delivered, reached up and touched the child on the head.

Ruth walked over and placed a clean piece of linen between the new mother's legs and moved up to stand beside the baby. "What you mean?" she asked, surprised but glad to hear Mattie speak.

"Maybe your God didn't hear. But I heard." She kept her eyes closed. The baby stilled upon her mother's belly.

"O live, child. O let this child live?" Mattie repeated the prayer she had heard her neighbor pray and then she whispered the baby's name as she fell back into the mouth of the river. "O live, Olivia."

Rise up ye Earth and speak the Truth
of Dark, of Light, of Pain
For the human tongue is slow to tell
what hands and hearts will stain.

Children play near open graves,
a fire so close they smell.
Prophecy loosens a stone cold heart
but cannot keep it from hell.

—ES

Three

Reverend Ely continued to function in means beyond himself. When Cy Gauldin mentioned in passing the young woman's delivery and the newborn infant who was not allowed to nurse, the Reverend walked to the store on his own initiative, bought a box of Carnation milk, and even rounded up bottles and nipples. All done without the prodding of church ladies or a written request from the county services agency.

Before he went to see Mattie and give her the things he had bought for the baby, he visited those touched by the fingers of the storm. He said prayers, listened to confessions, and even wiped the tears of the bereaved, all with appropriate warmth and professional empathy.

He drove old Miss Coble to the hospital and helped Willard Neese gather wood for his stove. He picked up medicine for little Floyd Dodder and took blankets to the gypsies. The tall, ungainly parson was known for his kindness and his quiet manner; and since he continued his acts of mercy, folks just thought Reverend Ely was carrying on. And though he never tried to hide his wounds, most of them did not attend to his slowed gait or the bandages wrapped around his hands.

Hardly anyone saw that just below the surface of his forced smile and wedged in between his words of pardon and assurance there raged a gaping hole. Thread pulling thread, the conviction of a clergyman began to unravel. Bit by bit, a small tear widened and frayed ends spread farther and farther apart exposing his already tattered soul.

Floyd Dodder recognized it; but his mother thought he was only acting feverish when he fought the words of Scripture the preacher tried to read. Marvella Coble saw the empty space; and believing that it represented the fast-approaching plane of death, she shouted out, "Dear Jesus," when the preacher reached for her. Ule Ubanavich, the old gypsy woman, tried to give him a small leather bag of roots and cloves of garlic to ward off evil spirits that loomed too near him, but he politely refused and she could not change his mind.

He felt the seams pull apart, but he only observed the colors and the textures of the narrow strings as they loosened and fell. He did not try to stitch them back together. He did not pray. He was not anxious or afraid. He only watched and counted as they slowly and painlessly untied and dangled near the edges of his heart. Losing his faith was the easiest thing he had ever done in his life.

Just before the November storm rolled through and silenced the world around Smoketown, Reverend Ely had gone to the shed behind the church to do a little cleaning. He walked through the back door, smiling to himself as he thought about the last time he had come to the old lean-to.

He remembered his own embarrassment and the looks of shock that he found when he had walked up on Becky Lee Meadows and Billy Disher.It didn't surprise him that the couple was there; he knew that this little building was where young Christians discovered sanctification in the forms of hand-rolled cigarettes, bottles of Randolph County moonshine, and underneath neatly ironed church dresses.

Once he realized whom and what he had come upon, he cleared his throat and turned his head while Becky Lee and Billy hurried to zip up his pants and button her sweater and then without a word rush through the door.

He spoke without sharpness or disappointment to their backs as they ran by, "See you both in church Wednesday night." With that, the incident was handled. And because of the kind of man he was, he never told a soul.

He was sweeping up bits of trash and cigarette butts on that cold, gray day when he saw an oval-shaped piece of glass and picked it up to look through. He held it up first to the ceiling and then to a knothole on the far wall and tilted it side to side, watching the folds and bends of reflected light. It was just as he was about to toss it out the door when he noticed the arm of the big oak tree.

His first thought was that a limb had cracked and was simply hanging low; and he held the piece of glass tighter, trying to see more clearly. He outlined the shape that dropped to only a few feet above the ground and paid no attention to the sharp edges cutting into his skin. He wanted to believe it was a limb. He tightened his grip, harder and deeper, trying to make the focus more or less clear. He spoke to himself out loud as if someone else might be listening, "It has to be a limb."

Streaks of red painted his oval window until he could no longer ignore the pain in his right hand nor the truth of what he saw. Still clutching the glass like it held the vision in itself, he walked toward the tree and faced the broken and battered body of Elton Williams. Tiny drops of blood marked the path from shed to tree and from life to death; and Reverend Ely stood without a prayer to the Christ he now believed was dancing in the palm of his hand.

For almost an hour alone and in the cold, the preacher sawed at the rope with his little piece of glass, trying to cut the young boy down. It did not occur to him to go and get a sharp blade or to yell for help. He did not think to run and call the police. There had been no plea to heaven. Already the threads were breaking and he cut them one by one with a dull, bloody shard of glass.

When the body fell, a thud on the frozen ground, Reverend Ely turned to the tree as if it were the murderer. In his mind he saw the tree lean its branches over to Mrs. Masie Williams's house and grab up Elton until he dangled from the arm of the killer like a charm. In an unexpected moment of passion, the pastor strove at the tree, kicking and hitting until he could no longer feel the tips of his fingers and toes. Then, exhausted from his attempt to kill a tree and bring justice to the murdered boy, he gathered the dead body in his arms and went inside the church to the altar.

He stayed there until the kerosene lamp burned out, without praying, even without weeping, just rocking the dead boy at the foot of the gold cross that stood in the center of the altar table.

He was trying to think of reason or cause that a boy had been hanged in the back of his sanctuary, trying to concentrate on the suffering Jesus and how the Messiah would have breathed life back into the child; he was trying to call on some means of comfort; but he had nothing, felt nothing, knew nothing, other than the unraveled place that exposed his shredded and disappearing faith.

After more than a couple of hours waiting on a silent God and trying to remember his sermon from the past week, the one for the following Sabbath, and thinking only of how small the gold cross had become, he emerged in the darkness, walked through Smoketown with Elton cradled in his arms until he found Mrs. Masie.

The mother of the dead boy fell hard across the path of sorrow. She did not pass easily through the valley of the shadow of her son's death. She grieved as only a murdered child's parent knows to grieve. But when folks looked back and remembered Mrs. Masie's bereavement, they would say Elton's mama did not take it as hard as the white preacher who, after finding and cutting down a black child who hung from a white boy's rope, landed deep into a pit of hopelessness and tried desperately to peel away his skin.

He walked to Mattie's early Sunday morning before church started when the ice was beginning to melt. With the boxes of milk and nipples beneath his arms, he strode without a sound to the small white shack and knocked on the door. His face was gray and marked with deep lines, his eyes dark with shadows; and although a bone was crushed in his right foot and three fingers were broken, he did not wince or favor them.

Roy opened the door and together they stood on opposite sides, the silence surprising or disturbing neither one. Ruth finally came from behind the little boy and welcomed the preacher into her neighbor's home. She felt the cord in her back tighten as an icy breath blew past her as he went into the front room on his left.

Tree and Olivia, both of them wide-eyed and curious, lay wrapped in blankets on the floor. Roy went around the preacher to join E. Saul over near the hearth of the wood stove where they had been playing. Ruth shut the door and turned to see the white gauze as it wrapped around the preacher's right hand and saw him shift his weight from right to left. His feet were wet from the walk. His eyes glassy and red from lack of sleep.

"You out awfully early this morning, Reverend." Ruth took a box from under his arm, trying not to stare. "Why not take off your shoes and set them by the fire? Your feet must be froze."

"I heard about Miss Jacobs and thought the milk might be helpful." He set the other box on the floor near the door and glanced over at the babies.

"Looks like she's already made a friend." He tried to put a

lift in what he said, but there was a cavernous ring to his voice. He sat down and began pulling off his shoes and socks.

Ruth saw the bruised foot, swollen and blue-black. She tried not to gawk but the size and depth of the wound disconcerted her. The preacher followed her eyes and he too became captivated by the part of his leg that hung from his ankle bone like a distended cloudy balloon.

The toes were folded, the tops skinned and patched in black. It was a neat and simple design that laced along the edges and dripped down into the cracks. It was purple where blood had gathered and dark blue like the night sky in winter just over the top where fragments of a bone lay shattered.

He traced the bruise, feeling no sensation or pain or tingling, just a deep numbness as he looked up, his face stern, and said to Ruth, "This is really nothing." And he stood up, placing his weight on the injured foot to prove himself, then set his shoes and socks near the stove.

There was another pause between them.

"I believe the storm has passed, Ms. Ruth. I hope you all did not suffer too much discomfort."

He sat down on the far right side of the sofa nearest to the hearth.

The hole in his voice and the bandaged hand and disfigured foot made Ruth wonder about which storm he spoke since they both knew two had raged across the region.

"No, sir, we all managed just fine. Course Mattie ain't come around since she labored. I worry a bit about her."

Ruth began telling the story of the birth, trying to find for herself at which point the woman faded into her dream. She walked out of the room and into the kitchen still talking while the children studied the face, the feet, and the hands of their guest.

Reverend Ely was no longer listening. He was no longer trying to be an entertaining visitor or even paying attention to what Ruth was saying. He was watching the breath of the wood heater. The climb and collapse of the red fingers that crawled up and down the inside of the belly. The patterned movement hypnotized the man; and the soothing warmth and perfect quiet made the preacher aware of his heaviness. In his eyelids and at the extensions of his wrists and legs. At the base of his brain and way beneath the softness of his heart muscle. Reverend Ely had been dogged by evil; and the rupture in his chest had finally stolen away his capacity to run.

Sleep came fast and easy; and by the time Ruth had finished her story and was bringing a cup of coffee into the room where he sat, the parson's face was to his chest, his arms hanging at his side.

All of his features relaxed. The angles rounded and the knots loosened. The needled expression he bore along his brow and down along his cheeks dulled; and his too-squared shoulders dropped and bowed. It was peaceful and he was tired. So he gave into himself and took rest. Rising and falling with the perfect timing of a flame.

Deeply and fully he slept, diving straight through the dream state and entering into an unplumbed coma. He was motionless, his heartbeat slowed, his lungs delayed. He had fallen completely into sleep. No tossing or turning, no struggle to stay awake. And as if he had been given a secret gift from angels, when he awoke, just fifteen minutes later, the nap was all he needed to see clearly.

He turned and looked about him. Everything was vivid. The curious awareness of wide blue eyes. A stream of dust along the top of a picture frame. The crimson belly that swelled and emptied. The tightness of a corner and the small yellow spots just above his head. The uneven strokes of a paintbrush along the walls and the tiny flowers on Ruth's apron. Violets, he said to himself. The pale stench of a baby's urine. The feel of smooth cotton. The bitter taste of coffee. The tractable clucking of a mother's tongue behind her teeth. Everything about his senses was sharp and fine-tuned.

He directed his clarity on things that were going on outside the house. He could hear the slush of ice against rubber. Blink at the too-bright sun that glistened on tin. Chill at the whip of a breeze as it struck the back of his neck. Everything was distinct and easily defined including even the precise absence of feeling in his foot and in his hands.

Ruth saw the change. She had not been bothered by his nap; she was glad the pastor could rest so easily in her presence. She was not troubled that he had fallen asleep for a brief time, but there was something unhinged about him since he woke up. A glint in the way he kept looking at things. A ferocity about his vision. A flash that happened too quickly as he went around the room focusing on colors or sounds or something she could not name. She was unsure of what he thought he was seeing and she was unsettled by his farsightedness.

"That Mattie's boy?"

It had been an awkward silence; yet he made no apology for sleeping and no attempt at light conversation to recover the lapsed time.

His question stunned Ruth and after a moment of hesitation she answered, "Yes, sir," deciding that a redirection of focus might take away from the sternness of her thoughts. "Roy, come and meet the preacher."

Roy moved slowly over to Ruth from behind the stove, pressing his back into her knees. She wrapped her arms around his shoulders and smiled down at the child.

"Good-looking boy, ain't he?"

E. Saul followed behind his friend, stopping just at his mother's side.

The Reverend had retrieved his socks and shoes and was putting them on. When he was finished he dropped to his knees right in front, eye level to the white boy. The clear-eyed man saw the crooked part in the little boy's hair and the smeared syrup dried and sticking to the corners of his mouth. He saw the blue space in the child's eyes and the look of misunderstanding so often confused for sadness. He saw the dirty lines just under his chin and the purple-red scar that wrapped around his neck. All of this he saw.

Then without touching the little boy, the man spoke, "Your

name Roy?" Their faces so close that they breathed each other's air.

Roy didn't answer, but he also didn't break the stare.

"Roy," Reverend Ely said in a rolling voice as he shook his head, "trees are the arms of God." His eyes were firm and unyielding. This was the sermon he was meant to preach.

"They can be strong and hearty, giving themselves so children can climb to housetop heights and swing from the lapis-lazuli sky to the emerald-green earth. They can be tall and solid like the mighty oak or delicate and wispy like the weeping willow and the silk tree. They can glory God with rainbow-colored leaves and little bitty pink and white flowers. They can bear fruit as sweet as full red cherries and as handsome as the crisp apple and the ripe yellow pear. Nuts that crack open spilling a fresh and tasty meat."

His singsong voice floated and fell, twirling like a seed in spring air.

"They will shade you in the summer, a cool resting place to lean your tired back, give you music as the wind whispers through the spiny fingers that dance above your head. All these things and more," the preacher said without moving his eyes from the face of the child, "can these creatures give to us." It was perfect, every word, every inclination, every rise and fall of his voice. He was in love with his own gift.

"They were made to enjoy and be enjoyed and that, my little friend, they will do. But, Roy"—he reached up and dropped his hands on the boy's shoulders, the sermon now heading in a new direction, a way of admonition and warning—"don't ever, no matter how twisted and torn your life may get, don't ever use a tree to do your evil." The pause was severe.

"Trees are the arms of God." And he touched Roy's neck, causing the boy to step back and snap up his head.

Ruth handed the preacher his hat and coat and he smiled and walked through the door, shielding his eyes from the brightness of the morning and the clarity of what he knew was going to happen next. He went to church relieved.

When the time for the sermon came the Reverend Ely got up and faced the congregation. They had softened in their seats and now awaited the Word, interpreted and spoon-fed in such a way that it could sit easily in their mouths, slide painlessly down into their cold rock bellies, and fill them up with comfort.

They had sung the gentle hymns, heard the announcements, read together one of the stories of Jesus, an easy one of bearable and uncostly love; and they were pleased with how the hour was going. It was the service of worship they had created and sacrificed to keep in place.

There were four other preachers who came and went before Reverend Ely took the job, each of them fired because of unsolicited expectations for the rural church. They hired Reverend Ely, a retired schoolteacher, after three years of an empty pulpit only because he said that he would charge them for just the preaching and not for the visiting or Bible study and because he did not have a long-term mission plan for the membership growth.

He was held in only modest regard by most of the members

of Pinetops Baptist Church. They all thought he was a little too book smart and a bit too involved with the people of Smoketown; but at least he had not arrived with grandiose ideas of worshiping with the Methodist Church or getting caught up in community outreach. And he had never, not in the ten years he had been their preacher, ever made an attempt to change the order of service.

As he stood to preach on that bright November Sunday morning, the ice melting and the sun high and strong, he looked around at who was in attendance at church. He paid attention to which members had braved the cold and come to worship in such a short time after the falling of the first winter storm.

The Walkers were there, on the third row just as faithful as rain. Mr. and Mrs. Harvey sat near the back with John Gaston, Sr., who was already dozing, and the Bentley twins, whom no one could tell apart. Edith and Becky Lee sat struggling with itchy wool and too many clothes while Effie and Lacy Finch adjusted themselves so that Miss Agnes Withers would not block their view. He studied them all as they fidgeted in the silence, moving quietly from face to face.

He stopped, however, when he got to the center of the sanctuary. Reverend Ely locked his vision, found his mark; and it was on the fifth row evenly spaced from left to right where his sermon began.

Leroy Johnson did not hit his children. He never laid a hand upon his wife. He had always been silent as stone. His heart just as hard, but he did not define his violence in physical terms.

For him, it was in the way he cut his eyes and left a room, the way he finished a sentence, brutal and abrupt. He worked his boys like they were mules with the only show of affection being the nod he gave their way when one outlasted the other in the fields, working with the livestock, or in fair fights.

The three boys learned that their father would share with them only what he must, shelter, food, and an intolerance for anyone different from themselves. He bred the quality of bigotry in his family like it was royal blood; and he wished nothing more than for his children to nurture that quality and give it life in ways he never could. With only the common desire to please their father, the three boys looked for means by which to claim his blessing.

It was no surprise then to any of the three when the black boy stopped breathing. They knew with only a glimpse that the defiant black youth who would not run away with his friends must bear the consequences of their family's stock. And when he would not scream out or beg them to stop, reminding them of their father's silent desires, it only made the blows come harder, the kicks more frequently.

He was dead when they hanged him, but to the three white brothers it was not over until they ritualized their feelings and brought fear to an entire community. The black boy hanging from a tree in the back of their church was the shrine to their father who taught them how to hate.

Reverend Ely looked down the row of the Johnson family and recognized the blood of Elton Williams as it spread across their consolidated vacant gaze. Even Beulah, who did not birth the prejudice, nursed it with her milky compliance, dripping blood from her hands as if it were she who stood by the tree and tied the knotted noose. It had taken the whole family to create this act of evil. But more, it involved the entire congregation of Pinetops who gave permission for this to occur on their property. It was the act of the whole town, the whole race that nodded its head in approval by not saying a word.

He watched the blood spill into the aisle as the old women struggled to keep the stains from their shoes and old men danced about avoiding puddles. Higher and higher the sea of red rose until Reverend Ely knew of only one sacrament to rid them of this blight.

He walked down the steps to the altar mumbling some words and then knelt at the table. There was an uncomfortable sway in the congregation as necks strained to grant focus to what the man was doing since never in the decade of his preaching had he ever left the pulpit.

With both hands he yanked up the candle placed near the center next to the offering plates and stepped back into the pulpit. Holding the stick like a sword he lit the pages of the Bible and waited until the blaze stood high and white red before he dropped his blood-soaked face into it like it was a holy baptism. The fire crackled and hissed as a man of the cloth disintegrated within its hot arms. The preacher never said a word, his sermon burning through the sanctuary, hot and winding.

The Sunday morning gatherers hurried from their seats, watching from a distance as the old church smoldered, leaving nothing in its place but a golden cross and a smooth piece of oval glass that finally popped and shattered, dropping into the ashes of a man whose vision was blemished by guilt.

Shoestring Cannon had been huddled near the rear of the church when he smelled the fire. It did not alarm or frighten him; it merely motioned like a fat crooked finger, leading him up the steps and out past the choir room where he saw a Bible engulfed in flames and a preacher laugh and kiss the lips of hell.

The hobo was sure that this was Satan's doing. He knew that Reverend Ely, who had let him in the back door to get warm, had been possessed by demons since all those in church reported that he had not said a prayer all morning. The old man was also certain that the whole area was cursed by the devil's smoke and that anywhere that the soot or gray mist settled there would be trouble and misfortune.

In Shoestring's mind, the fact that only a cross was left was sign from the gates of purgatory that all those in the vicinity must beg for the Lord's forgiveness or hell would surely swallow them. And with that notion he deemed as prophecy, the man with the limber back and raw-boned arms helped the members put out the fire and then ran through the street calling for sinners to repent and save themselves from destruction.

When the crazed man ran by Ruth and the boys who were standing behind the front screened door of Mattie's house, he saw the ashes spread along the porch and steps. He stopped and licked his finger, yelled out the preacher was dead, and made a cross in the air trying to protect them from the spirit of death that would not pass over a dwelling stained with the markings of Hades.

Ruth pulled the boys away and closed the door, the fire truck clanging up the hill. She checked out the window, making sure the fire was contained and that she and her neighbor were safe from the burning, and remembered the Reverend Ely's visit and the glaze that reached behind his eyelids and covered his stare. She thought about his final words to Roy, something about trees, and how even after the nap, even after he was rested and refreshed, he had seemed as off-centered as the old railroad man spitting crosses in the wind.

Ruth went to the back bedroom to check on Mattie and found her, eyes open, face upward, her arms folded across her belly as if she were resting in her grave. "Well, look who's finally woke up."

Mattie turned and peered toward the door, her face gaunt and knotted. "What's happened?"

"Well, what you wanna know first?" She sat in a chair next to the bed. "The fire is Pinetops; burning down this morning. You had a baby on Friday, and we ain't heard a word from you since."

"I had a baby?" Mattie put her hand beneath the cover feeling for a sign of birth. She ran her fingers down her swollen belly and felt the sticky clots of blood that had pooled between her legs. "You been here all this time?"

Ruth straightened the hem of her dress. "Mama came and stayed a while yesterday while I did some laundry; but yeah I been here."

Mattie closed her eyes. "It was quite a dream." And she pulled back the sheets and started to stand. Stiff towels fell from between her legs as she wobbled at the quick change of positions.

Ruth stood up to help by taking her arm and they walked to the front room together. She gathered some clean rags that were hanging in the kitchen for Mattie to sit on as the young woman leaned slowly onto the sofa. Olivia was hungry and Mattie motioned for the baby. Ruth handed her the child and watched the ease with which she fed her.

She unbuttoned her blouse and set her baby near to her breast. It was startling to Mattie to feel the sucking of something so hungry and after a while when the milk began to run, she thought she saw her lover's face pour from her nipple in a long, creamy white line. She watched the baby curl her hands and then stretch her wrists and saw the muscles that gathered her mouth in a tight bow. She watched the swallowing in her neck.

The tug and hold on her left breast was both pleasurable and painful; but it was hardly meaningful to the woman who knew so little about tenderness. Ruth, however, believed in what she saw. A mother was feeding her child; and to a midwife, that was enough to sustain and nurture life.

The sucking noises offended Roy. The smack, smack, smack made him angry and he was sorry to see Mattie awake again. He had come to enjoy the presence of this new family and the absence of the old one. E. Saul taught him games and riddles while Ruth perfumed the house with rich smells of fruit pies and buttered bread that before had only hinted at him through broken glass.

She rubbed his neck with Vaseline that had taken away the

roughness of his scar. And she touched it without cringing, something no one else could do. He did not crouch in fear while they were there nor was he sent to his room before dark and forced to dive between quilts to keep from hearing these same kinds of sucking and smacking noises.

He had watched Ruth feed her baby. But she sang while she rocked; and the creaking of the chair and the low deep tones of her voice soothed away the hungry sucking of the baby. Soft as fur her songs would slide across the room and slow the gasps for air from the nursing child. Steady was the wood rolling on wood that kept the rhythm of a mother's song.

It was satisfying to sit near them, not like this. Not like the hard tow and drag of this woman's child. Roy got up and went into the kitchen with E. Saul quickly chasing him. Roy already missed his mother's death.

Olivia fell asleep cradled in Mattie's arms and was quickly returned to the floor next to Tree. Mattie reached behind her back and found a pack of cigarettes from a table drawer. She pulled one out, lit it, and took a breath, enjoying the taste of tobacco that seeped across her tonsils and down into her lungs.

"Roy, go get me a blanket," Mattie hollered past the door.

Roy slowly got up from the war zone in front of the kitchen stove where he and E. Saul were playing with bits of paper, making armies and tanks, and went into his mother's bedroom and pulled the old patched quilt from the bed. He dragged it into the sitting room and handed it to Mattie.

She reached down and touched his face. "You got to be so

big, Roy. I'd forgotten how blue your eyes is." He leaned away from her and returned to his game.

"So what started the fire?" Mattie peeked out the window and draped the quilt around her, enjoying the sweetness of the smoke that circled from inside her lungs to form a wall that thickened and grew above her head.

"Don't know," Ruth said as she rocked back and forth, peering out past the window. "I did hear that the preacher is dead. He come by this morning, you know."

"Yeah, what for; he looking to save me?" She moved over to the sofa.

"No, he brought some milk for the baby." Ruth glanced over at the boxes. "He acted a little touched, but I figured it was from the lynching."

"Who got hung?" Mattie tapped at the ashes of her burning cigarette.

"He found Elton Williams out at the oak just a few days before the storm. I believe that's what broke him. Folks say he carried the body all the way to Elton's mama, never stumbled or asked for help. But something just didn't seem right about him this morning."

Ruth tugged at her stockings. "He was a good man. I'm right sorry he had to die."

"Yeah, well enough of this death talk." Mattie put out the cigarette. "I'm starving; what is it that smells so good?"

There was a pause and she turned to Ruth who was frowning. "Oh, now, don't go looking at me like that. Ain't nothing I can do about it, is there?"

Ruth was shaking her head. "You could sit with it a minute. You white folks beat everything. Somebody die in the morning and you wanna get him in the ground by lunchtime. Can't you all just sit with it a minute? Just let your heart feel something for somebody else just a minute? Beat all I ever seen."

She yanked the towels up from the floor. "A church is burning to the ground, a preacher, who had a kind heart, is dead; and all you thinking about is eating." She made a low moaning sound of disapproval.

Mattie rolled her eyes like a child. "Okay, I'll sit with it; but while I do, can I get some lunch?" She grinned at her neighbor.

Ruth got up and slapped Mattie's leg. "Girl, you try me, you know that?"

They both laughed and Ruth went to the kitchen while Mattie tried but failed to sit with the pain. Someone else's misery just couldn't hold her consideration for any more than that of her own.

When the afternoon crept into the arms of dusk, Ruth and her children left. Roy watched his neighbors walk to their house from the chalky split panes in his room. With Mattie having returned from the dead, things would go back to the way they were before, except for the addition of this sucking, crying, wetting thing that took up his space by the stove and peered up to him for help.

E. Saul peeked over his shoulder and waved at the boy, but Roy only buried himself into the quilts, hoping that the double rings and the sunbursts would ease the loneliness that crawled up his spine and settled in his throat.

He dived in finding scraps of life in every panel of Kay Martha's old quilts. And Roy tried to step inside the patterns of daisies and moons and feel the colors like they were part of him. He imagined the slim needle lifting the stone yellow color from his legs and fixing it into a flower or a sliver of sunshine. He knew the blue would come from his eyes and patch up a stretch of the sky where he could disappear.

He spread himself from corner to corner, turning out rose and pink and stems of green-black and coffee-brown. He would float in and out of the colors as if he was nothing more than drops of light and could move into and out of the fabric with the ease of a keen silver point. Back and forth he would start to go, picking up speed, becoming lighter and lighter like the wisps of dye that beckoned him.

And he could almost fly off in weightless shaded ribbons, easily and casually, except for a throbbing unwieldy red ring that would not fade. It held him down like an anchor. And the boy watched from below as the moons and the daisies fluttered around and above him and vanished again into the darkness.

Mattie finished her meal and headed for the sofa. Olivia was ready to nurse and Mattie picked her up aware of the rip up and inside her legs that ached and burned. She hated what birth did to her body. The marks that stretched across her belly and down along her thighs. Her posture bent from the extra weight that lowered her shoulders and left her spine drooped. Lumpy tits, hardened from stones of milk, the tender nipples. The vacancy in her vagina where the ligaments had torn. The emptiness that it left her with, having grown so accustomed to the presence of another. The widening of bones and the loosening of skin.

She wanted to be young again. Tight muscles and lithe. Dancing wildly with strong ankles and hips. The twist in her neck, so fast. The firm breasts that had never been handled. The chill of her tongue from ice cream or dirty talk. The quick stab of a pebble on the pads of her feet that had not grown callused and leathery. The surprise of water splashing on unexposed skin. The snug waist and taut buttocks that she could squeeze together and hold a dime. The goose-bumped unknowingness of what the body could do and the eagerness to try anything from backward flips off a landing to pulling down her panties and letting Tommy Logan feel her for a penny.

Everything felt old to her. Used up and done too many times before. And even though she still enjoyed sex, it was only because she liked the noises and the mixing of smells. Liquor and sweat. Tobacco and her moisture. Grunts and graphic descriptions of what felt good, the satisfaction at the shrivel of a man when he was done. But that was the most of her sensory pleasures. Alcohol dulled her and childbirth stole her brawn.

"You shot through me like a bullet, little girl," she spoke to the feeding child edged between her breast and a pillow. "And you out here now like you wanted so bad." Mattie lifted her breast making the feeding easier.

"I reckon you'll see it ain't such a wonderful thing to be born. Can't imagine that the joy of living ever wipes away the longing. But you here now."

The tiny infant stared up at her mother.

She leaned forward to the coffee table and picked up the pack of cigarettes. She pulled one out and lit it. The trail of smoke curled around her lips. She peered down at her daughter.

The baby closed her eyes, then opened them again.

She touched the baby on the forehead, tracing her finger along the infant's brow. She took a long, slow drag from the cigarette, then crushed it in the ashtray beside her. She nodded off while Olivia watched her sleep. The baby smiled at the dark-haired woman who fed her but did not see. And the light from fire and heaven dimmed in the night shadows as mothers and children everywhere hoisted themselves onto the dreams of each other.

You my best friend
(clap together clap)
Sisters to the very end
(legs slap, slap)
I'll go where you gone
(snap fingers snap)
Never ever be alone
(toes tap, tap)

Keep you covered from the rain
(clap together clap)
Protect you from your mama's pain
(legs slap, slap)
Through thick and thin, we more than friends
(snap fingers snap)
We sisters to the very end
(toes tap, tap)

Four

Witchhazel Comely lived only about a mile from the field that used to be a church, now empty of ash or steeple. It just seemed farther because it was way back in the woods where pine trees, thick and tall, circled her rickety old chimney that was always breathing fire.

Witchhazel grew herbs and knew recipes for every ailment that had come up in the ninety or so years she had been gardening cures. She had love potions and tonics for grief. She could made soft soap and pastes for removing stains. She blew out burns and talked off warts. And there was even a story that she raised a boy from the dead. She was known far and wide for her salves and teas; and folks, black and white, sent out after her assistance when harm took hold of a body.

She lived alone except for her dog named Gabriel. And she never left her house in the woods except twice, once in 1904 when the mayor was bleeding at the lungs and a second time when she lifted herself from off her own deathbed and walked to the edge of Smoketown, having recognized the third passing of evil just as it was making its way across a garden path.

In 1904, Mrs. Emily Murphy had tried the town doctor and had even sent off for the one in Winston-Salem, but no one could keep the mayor from declining. Finally, Johnnie Mays, a devoted house servant who was frustrated at his employer's distress, told her about Witchhazel and how she was blessed with the Gift. Mrs. Emily Murphy, without so much as a question, immediately sent him to fetch her.

Witchhazel told the young dark man that she never left her house, that she would give the herbs and the needed instructions; but that she never left and she wasn't about to start for no white man. And then she jerked her head like a punctuation mark and went inside. Johnnie Mays ran across town from the mayor's house to Witchhazel's three times before coming up the fourth time riding a carriage and convinced her to come out of the woods and into the tidiest part of Greensboro.

Some folks said it was on account of the money that Mrs. Emily Murphy offered; but everybody knew that Witchhazel had no use for money and only took food and corn liquor for payment. A couple of people counted it was the threat the mayor's wife ordered that she would be run out of town; but Witchhazel wasn't scared of anything living or dead; so most everyone agreed she went because of that carriage that Johnnie Mays came riding up in.

It was a shiny black carriage with six, not four, not two, dark red horses with eyes as bright as dawn and coats as glossy as mahogany wood. They stepped with high curved legs that struck the air with distinction and dropped to the ground in a small swirl of dust. Their manes, combed and smooth, were straight strands that glistened without a tangle; and their hooves were polished and tan, spawning no chips or unsightly smirch.

Witchhazel rode high in the seat, her aged black felt hat cocked to one side. Gabriel sat next to her, the straggly mutt that howled at first moons; and even though he was only a dog, held his head in dignity while sniffing the smells that rose up from below him. The old woman rode through the town like the Queen of Heaven and stayed seated until Johnnie Mays jumped from the driver's bench and went around to help her down. When she got inside the house, going through the front door, Mrs. Emily Murphy hurried her to her husband's side, begging her to save him.

Witchhazel gave the mayor three different remedies that she mixed up in a bowl by the bed. She grounded dry persulfate of iron into a fine powder and held it up to his nose until he breathed it all in. Then she gave him raw table salt to eat and finally an hour later fed him three teaspoonfuls of powdered loaf sugar and resin.

The mayor's wife watched the large black woman as she pulled the ingredients from an old leather bag that she wore on her back. And it was Mrs. Emily Murphy herself who brought Witchhazel a sandwich while the servants shook their heads in disbelief at the woman who would not let them speak to her without first saying "mam."

When Witchhazel was all done and satisfied with her work, she climbed back up into that carriage with Gabriel; and Johnnie Mays quickly drove her home. She left enough persulfate and raw table salt for four more doses and explained to the mayor's wife at exactly what time to administer them.

Mrs. Emily Murphy had handed her a crisp one-dollar bill; but Witchhazel rolled her eyes and motioned it away, pointing to a new green velvet hat that hung in the foyer that Mr. Murphy had gotten for Christmas. That and a sack of flour was all she took.

One week later the mayor was back in his office and Witchhazel never had a lack of food or liquor since.

Tree had to wait until she was seven years old before she and Olivia could walk the path to Witchhazel's house without E. Saul or Ruth holding their hands. It was not a long walk or even dangerous, but there was a short and tempting detour that led to Sticky Ledbetter's still, which was often a place where poker led to knife fights and more than dancing went on behind the shed.

Sticky had a deal worked out with Les Narron, the sheriff, so complaints or reports to the law always fell on deaf ears. And since it was actually over in Smoketown, it was not much of a threat to Les or the department that was responsible primarily to the citizens on the other side of the burned-down church.

It was the first day of summer, not according to the calendar, but according to children who sat at the edge of their desks with shoes rubbing too tightly on itchy feet and faces wiped way too clean. They waited in reckless anticipation for school to be over. Teachers struggled for attention in competition with tractors and blue jays; and they too watched the clocks for the exact moment when freedom rang. When school ended for the year, summer began. Not before or after.

Olivia and Tree had already made great plans for the hot days, the long and lazy afternoons after chores and without homework. They had both found it difficult when they started school one year earlier and had to be separated. Neither one of them had yet to realize that they went to different schools because of their color. They thought it was just a line that somebody drew dividing the two schools' populations.

Everybody up from Olivia's house went to a new brick building called Alamance School and everybody down from Tree's house went to an old barn built on a tobacco field, simply known as the Farmschool. Since the division came between them, the two little girls just assumed that there was a line down beneath the earth running straight between their houses marking school districts. And although they met and played every day after school, summer meant making up for all the lost time that the invisible line stole from them.

Before the final day of school, Ruth made a list to give to Witchhazel that she stuck inside Tree's front pocket of her bib overalls and then snapped them with snaps on both sides. With strict instructions about going nowhere near Sticky Ledbetter's wood shack and staying clear of the Mudbank Creek that was a breeding place for copperheads and water moccasins, Tree hurried off to school trying to make the hours go faster.

When the day was finally over Tree ran all the way home, beating everyone from the Farmschool and meeting Olivia just as she turned the corner from Alamance. They dashed to Tree's house, dropped off their things from the last day of school, grabbed a biscuit from the table, and headed out front. Miss Nellie yelled something about slamming doors; but Tree and Olivia were already well on their way, down past Tincan Gentry's house, and crossing the street into the garden beside the church cemetery, the garden everybody called Gethsemane.

A small patch of land Gethsemane was named by the women at The Ashley Grove Church, AME Zion Congregation, that was just across the road. They called it that because there were four short rows of sunflowers that grew every year and stood like tall crooked bodies with faces to the sky looking radiant but sleepy, dropping their heads hard and long just as the sun lowered. They reminded everyone of the disciples who fell asleep when Jesus was praying and were used more than once as an illustration in a preacher's sermon.

There was a bench behind the flowers and Tree and Olivia stopped to finish their biscuits and decide the best way to go to Witchhazel's.

Although they intended to stay on the path, when they got close to Sticky Ledbetter's place they heard laughter and singing that stopped them in their tracks, turning their heads away from the clear and straight way and toward the sweetness that drifted up from the still. It was easy from there. They simply followed the hum of voices and the sugary smells and ended up just twenty feet from the wood shack.

They giggled at the danger and when Tree darted ahead to a large mound of dirt, Olivia sat down and emptied her shoes of the pebbles that were pressed between her toes and causing her discomfort.

"Livia, Livia, get up and come here. Livia!"

Tree suddenly realized that the adventure was cut short by her friend's absence and she was feeling a bit too vulnerable to be so near the still by herself. Though she thought she should move back closer to Olivia, she was also drawn for just a closer look at this "Den of Iniquity" that caused her grandmother to rant at the devil and spit out Scripture with a vengeance.

This was the place her mother had said men go to piss away their families' earnings and women go to piss away their families.

Tree peeked from behind the mound of dirt and heard the voices of a man and a woman as they came from the front of the shack and walked to a spot just a few feet away from the little girl. Tree sucked in her breath as she heard a light low voice that was both strange and familiar and she froze in fear that the man and the woman would realize that they were not alone.

She knew that they were just on the other side of the mound that kept her hidden; and when she finally decided to take a quick look over on the other side she saw a hand reach around and almost touch her leg. That was when she noticed the fingers. Long, slender fingers, white as pearls with sharp red tips that dug at the dirt, grabbing and pulling, trying to hold on.

"Damn it, Willie, you're hurting me, ain't you ever heard of letting a woman get ready?"

"Not when I'm paying for it," came the gruff reply.

Tree was frozen. If she moved they would surely hear her. If Olivia came any closer she would see her mother participating in the most abominable act that seven-year-old girls can fathom. She watched the pearl hand scrape at the ground, tear at the side of her wall, and then fall limp, palm open as the red-tipped fingers curled and dropped.

"Hardly worth three dollars, you cheap cunt."

"Well if you lasted longer than three minutes, maybe you'd get your money's worth."

There was a rustle of clothing and Tree watched as the hand slid around the dirt. She counted to twenty, a secret she learned from her grandmother, a method to think before acting. And then she jumped from her seat and ran until she found where Olivia was putting on her shoes. She grabbed her up and the two of them began pushing through thornbushes, jumping over logs, and dodging low-hanging limbs.

"Tree, slow down, Tree! What's the matter with you?" Olivia fought to stay at the heels of her friend.

Tree didn't stop running until she was at a clearing that was on the road heading into the grove of pine trees, away from the creek and away from Sticky Ledbetter's. Then she dropped from the waist down, her head facing the ground, her arms holding her sides.

Gasping for breath she said, "Won't nothing. I just, uh, I just didn't want that man to see us."

Olivia laughed and threw a rock at her friend's feet. "You crazy, you know that? I almost lost my shoes chasing after you."

She fell into the small grassy area. Tree smiled and sat down next to her and they both laid back and watched the sun play in the tops of the pines.

Tree narrowed her eyes at the green that split and shattered in the sky and tried to forget what she had seen and heard. Mattie was one of those women. For three dollars she had allowed a man to enter her, to touch her in the warm and mysterious place where babies waited to be born. For three dollars she had opened herself to a man who called her names and did not love her openness.

Most of what Tree knew about sex came from Geneva Gentry. Geneva had seen her daddy riding her mother like a horse and said that it was a horrible, painful thing that had made her mother cry and scream out. Ruth had tried to convince her that sometimes it wasn't bad, but it should never be done unless you were in love.

It was a gift Tree's mother had said, and must be respected, never given without thought and prayer. And although she had tried to explain the beauty of intercourse, Tree clung to the story of a man mounted on a woman, who now clutched at the earth for forgiveness. She was now filled with shame as well as an overwhelming sense of responsibility for her friend.

She would never tell Olivia. She would never tell anyone. This was the secret she would keep to her grave; and she promised such a thing to the sky and the sun and the parting of green above her head.

"You my best friend, Olivia."

"Nah, Tree, you and me, we sisters."

"Yeah," Tree said, stretching it out like a yawn. "Through thick and thin, we more than friends, we sisters."

Olivia smiled, remembering Miss Nellie's rhymes that she would sing while the two girls played near her.

"I know what let's do." Tree sat up, the idea lifting her spirits. "Old Lady Witchhazel got potions for everything. Maybe she's got something that can really make us sisters."

"You mean like cutting our fingers and mixing the blood? I know some boys at school who did that. They made themselves a boys' club and say no girls allowed."

Olivia rose to her feet, slinging her shoes behind her head. "Like that, you mean?"

"Yeah. Something that nobody can take from us; something nobody will know about but us. Something that can make us so close that nobody will ever come between us." Tree took off her shoes going barefooted like Olivia.

"Well, let's go then."

Olivia was already up and heading toward the smoky cabin at the end of the path when Tree came up behind her. "Last one's a rotten egg!" And she hurried off ahead of her friend.

"Oh, yeah?" Olivia yelled to Tree as she slowed down. "First one's got to eat it!" And then she ran to catch up.

There were squeals and laughter when the two girls finally made it to the steps at the porch. Gabriel lifted his head, then dropped it again to the ground without even sniffing what he already knew was not dangerous. Tree knocked on the door with great enthusiasm while Olivia peeked in through the window, careful not to step on Gabriel's tail.

"I'm coming! Lord, there better be a fire or Judgment Day for this much racket!" But no fire or messiah stood at her door, just two sweaty girls, barefoot and grinning.

"You children lost?" Witchhazel opened the door.

"No, mam. I come for some things for my mama. She say she'll send E. Saul over with a quail later on for pay."

Witchhazel motioned them in and the two friends walked through the door, taking in the sights and the smells just as they had when they came with Ruth on their first visit.

The cabin was an extension of the forest that surrounded it. There was a woodsy odor that permeated through the walls and down along the floorboards. There were scents of camphor and orange flowers, jasmine and cloves. And there was, as always, an iron pot that bubbled and stewed like a witch's brew, hanging over the fire in a fireplace cut into the far wall.

Roots hung from the ceiling away from the fire; and the old medicine woman had her own way of telling them apart. Bags of yellow straws and baskets of dried flowers stood in corners and out along the porch. There were paper sacks tied with strings that were marked with small zigzag lines drawn with the burnt end of a stick. These were placed along a shelf that wrapped around the house and stood high above the little girls' heads.

Neither the place nor the woman frightened Olivia and Tree, but they were careful not to touch or disturb anything around them. They knew Witchhazel could take away aches and get rid of fever. They knew she could cure the colic and soothe coughs and spider bites. They had seen her teas put babies to sleep and old men back to walking; and they both had experienced her healing on a firsthand basis. But they also knew she could make stuffed dolls that looked like somebody. And she could squeeze the small toy until the look-alike person vomited or had large bruises on the inside of their thighs or down along their spines. They knew that if she got a lock of your hair or a fingernail she could boil it in salt water and bury it and worms would eat away your stomach and liver.

It was common knowledge to most folks who abided by Witchhazel's cures that not everything that she knew about herbs and roots was of a healing nature. But even knowing these things, Olivia and Tree were not afraid of her. They merely respected her and her dwelling with the same reverence and mystery that they took with them to church or a graveyard.

"You Ruth's girl?"

Tree was studying the recently acquired pieces of slippery elm bark that were spilled out on the table near the fire. "Yes, mam."

"Your mama let you come by yourselves?" Witchhazel enjoyed their curiosity.

"Mama say it fine now that me and Olivia is seven years old." Tree spoke with a certain amount of pride that brought a smile to the old woman's lips.

"So you must be Olivia." Witchhazel had seen the little white girl before when Ruth had come with the two of them, but she had never spoken to her. "And you seven too, huh?"

"Yes, mam." Olivia turned away.

"Well, you gonna tell me what your mama want or am I 'spose to guess?" Witchhazel was eating pumpkin seeds, spitting the shells into a pile near the stove.

There was a second while the two girls looked at each other in a state of puzzlement when Tree remembered the list in her pocket and quickly gave it to Witchhazel.

"That chickweed and mugwort stop the swelling in your granny's feet?" Witchhazel was studying the list. Tree shrugged her shoulders.

The old woman could not read anything except the names of the flowers and herbs she used. She had started getting lists about thirty years ago when people began to know what to ask for. So she memorized the way they looked written down just as she learned how to find them growing in a field or near a creek bank. She observed the loops and hooks in letters the same way she mastered the feel of prickly leaves and the differences between tree barks and brown mosses.

She had even learned the spelling of her own name when Elsie Luther had all her teeth pulled and sent her son, JW, to fetch some witch hazel for her sore gums. The old medicine woman had listened to JW as he read off the list and then looked at it herself to see the doubled dip in the first letter and the likeness in the two in the middle, sitting side by side. She was proud of the way that there were two words molded into one, each made with five units, and how the whole name ended with a very tall and a very straight line stretching from top to bottom.

She traced the word over and over in the dust on the floor, with a stick along the ground. And with her finger dipped in honey, she watched her name dry upon the table, golden and thick as she joined the two words together and christened herself with a gilded baptism.

"Let's see, castile soap and black cohosh, mormon tea and comfrey? Who at your house got hay fever?"

Tree thought for a minute and remembered her brother's sneezing and runny nose. "E. Saul."

"Well, tell your mama to feed him a little bee pollen. I'll put some in your bag. I got everything except for your flaxseed. Lotus DeVaughn bought all I had last Thursday." Witchhazel pulled out a small stool and stepped up to the shelf and picked out four small bags and dropped them on the table while she stood looming over her guests. "You girls need anything else?"

Olivia shifted closer to Tree, both dropping their eyes to the floor and putting their hands in their pockets. They walked over to the old woman as she stepped down from her perch.

Tree was the one to speak. "Well, yes, mam." She spoke slowly. "Well, I mean Mama don't, but we was wondering about something."

Witchhazel pushed the stool back against the wall waiting for the request. "Well," she said with a certain amount of impatience.

The little girl spoke hesitantly. "See, me and Olivia, well, we feel like sisters; and well, we thought maybe you had a potion or something that we could swallow that would really make us sisters."

Olivia joined in. "We could bring you flowers or something. We can't catch no bird."

Witchhazel stared at the little girls trying to remember her own childhood and how it felt to be so small. But Olivia's face stared back with a whiteness that kept pushing Witchhazel from any youthful memory.

She was touched by such a request, especially since few folks called upon her magic anymore. Most people simply used her as a pharmacist, not even needing her assistance in diagnosing illnesses or prescribing medications. Most everyone, by this time, ascertained the problem on their own and just needed Witchhazel to fill a bag with the herbs whose properties they understood but whose bloom or leaf they could never find.

But she was also aware that this request was weighty and too challenging to meet. She knew that sisters were hard to come by and completely unavailable when the skins were different. She didn't know whether to laugh or cry at the naïveté of seven-year-old girls, the sincerity, the innocence.

It was sweet, she admitted to herself, best friends playing like time was just another child who rolled down the grassy hills and fell into their arms like each other or swam near them in the cool spaces in rock quarries, jumping hand in hand into blue lake water high from a stony ledge.

It was uncomplicated to children. Always had been. Always would be. But it was not children who made the rules or enforced the boundaries. And even though it seemed impossible to two small girls in love with the world and each other, one day it would change. And one would be white and one would be black and no potion or cream, no poultice or filtered tea, would stop the hating that took on a pale complexion and separated them like a steep angry wall.

Witchhazel quit believing a long time ago that there would ever be a change; and the only reason she let a white person step through her door was the fear of what might happen. Not to her, she was starting to believe what people said about her, that nothing could kill her. No, it was the others she opened her door for. Only one thing worse than a white man; and that's a white man riddled with disease or pain.

That's why she went to the mayor's house. Not because of money or promise of food or evil. It wasn't even those six dark red horses or the tall black carriage that persuaded her to go. It was because of the savage desperation that she saw in Johnnie Mays's eyes on that fourth time at her door. She knew Mrs. Emily Murphy would start ripping backs or demanding bricks from straw if the mayor was not healed. So she went and nursed him back to life to save the salaries and the loose dignity of a white man's servants.

And now these two little girls were coming to her talking about being sisters. One white, who would one day choose her whiteness over her best friend, and one black, who would be forced to forget anything other than her dark reflection that stared back at her from mirrors and clear water, unforgiving faces, and closed doors.

There was something else, though. Something in the black girl's eyes. Something of urgency and the need to protect. There was some secret that heightened the need for a blessing. Some guarded knowledge that separated them and yet drew them again into each other. It was deep and pressing; and just like the plea of Johnnie Mays it wrestled beneath the eyelids of a black person and begged for the old woman's touch.

She surprised herself at even entertaining such a notion.

"Sisters?" She had moved to a chair at the table. "Where'd you get such a curious idea?"

Tree spoke for the two of them. "It was mine."

"Your'n? Well it's sweet, but I ain't got nothing for such a thing. Go on home now and get your mama these herbs."

Tree and Olivia stayed where they were. Witchhazel placed the little bags into one larger bag and handed it out to Tree. The little girl did not move toward the old woman or her outstretched arm.

"Ain't you got nothing?"

"It's silliness, girls. Pure silliness. You friends enough, you don't need no magic."

Tree slipped her hand into Olivia's. "We just want something to make it so."

Witchhazel sighed and turned in the chair until she was facing the window.

The flowers grew in bunches and crept along the ground from shade to shade, overgrown in kudzu and pigweed. It was ugly then; the flowers puny from unsplit bulbs that lay beneath the earth. Mites and spiders making homes in the unkempt garden while snakes drew comfort in the tall grass and thick ivy that wound around itself in poison.

There was no order or delineation. Tawny weeds toppled herb and crushed the roominess that used to welcome long florid displays and wide tongues of vegetation. Sticks hammered the soil and brown stole away the brightness that used to reach into her window.

It had been a long time since the windflowers, blue with black centers, melted into the lavender-pink glory of the snowflower. It seemed forever since the lips of her yard were traced in the dark orange-red of Apeldoorn tulips that lifted her garden into a smile. Years and lives had passed since Witchhazel's backyard had been a showplace of brilliance. Streaming in rows like a rainbow. And she looked out across the dull and weakened brown, the spiky callused green, and could not dismiss the dreams of little girls.

"This is very serious what you asking." The old woman did not turn from the window. "It means you vowing your love to each other, trusting and believing in each other, letting nothing nor nobody come between you. I 'spect it's more than you know." And she watched a butterfly spin across the spotted patches of grass, a burst of brilliance in a track of lazy boredom.

"Yes, mam." Tree and Olivia answered together.

"It ain't likely to work being the wrong time of the year and all. This is a harvest thing you asking. Meant to bind two people together before the heavy storms; ain't likely to work now." Witchhazel was speaking to the loose spaces in her heart.

The two girls stayed there, ready, faithful, waiting for instruction.

"Well, go on to the yard and draw a circle around the both of you with room enough for me to step in. Then stand in the circle with your foreheads pressed together, your hands to your sides. And this is the most important part." Witchhazel turned to face them, dead-eyed and tight-lipped.

"You must try as hard as you can till you can feel the other girl inside you. Knowing her breath for your own, her voice, her seeing, everything that's hers is yours. That's what you have to do for this ceremony to work."

There was a hushed silence as the two girls thought about their assignment. A moment of suspicion or doubt as to whether it was even necessary since they thought they already knew everything about the other. Now this woman was suggesting that there might be more.

Tree turned her eyes away from Witchhazel, who was now staring at her. If such a thing was possible, how could she keep the secret of Mattie from spilling out into the searching mind of Olivia? It was something she had not planned and now struggled with whether to stop the process before it ever began. But there was Olivia who was even more intrigued now that mystery was added to the ritual.

"You still interested?" Witchhazel saw the hesitation.

Olivia was the one to speak, "Yes, mam."

And she pulled Tree by the arm, through the door, and out into the backyard. She was also the one who drew the circle with her bare heel while Tree stood in the center and watched. Then she stepped inside.

"Well, you ready?" Olivia was red and glowing. She stood directly in front of her best friend and leaned into Tree. Tree pushed forward as well until the resistance was evened and they were steadied by the leverage. They closed their eyes and began.

It seemed forever before Witchhazel made her way to the backyard with Gabriel following closely behind her, dropping to the ground with only a limited amount of interest. The old woman examined the circle and the two girls and listened to the hums and buzzes of insects searching for a new leaf or petal.

Olivia and Tree stood eye to eye, their brows knitted tightly showing a great amount of determination. A light wind stirred in the pine tops; and there was an air of expectation as the afternoon deepened into low sticky skies that entertained no thought of rain.

She walked around the two girls, first left then right, and back again. Then she sprinkled them with rosewater that freshened and surprised them but did not bring them out of their stance. Witchhazel stepped outside the circle and began changing the direction which she faced, first to the east and then to the west, spouting out words that neither girl would later recall.

And then she danced.

Not in a fit of ecstasy or drunkenness but rather in a slight and methodical manner that was remembered in the muscles of the old woman's legs and in the arches of her feet. Her fingers sampled the air while her shoulders swayed and shrank. Her back, broken and healed, broken and healed, raised and lowered in an easy dip, her body, one black, graceful sail.

It was an ancient dance of women, celebrated when the men held council beyond the ears of wives and sisters. The domineering rite of exclusiveness turned into a ritual of joy. She touched her own face and the corners of her mouth, laughing to herself. Laughing at the power. Laughing at the magic. Both of which shivered between her legs and spread up inside her lungs in a warm spray of sunlight.

The music was clear and lovely; and Witchhazel straddled the tribal melody and set out across the sky.

Tree and Olivia, webbed inside the memories of slaves and healers, mothers and daughters, African and American, swallowed the past and waited for the present.

Olivia felt the shower of roses splash her face and the back of her neck, and she summoned the spirit of her friend as it rested upon her skull. She reached out for it, wanted it, welcomed it. And that's why when it fell down into her chest, she was stunned but did not gasp at its weightiness.

Before that moment, Olivia had never thought much about her best friend being black. It was never something that seemed to tie Tree down or keep her from doing anything that she wanted to do. Of course, they had both seen the places that were for whites only, but it didn't occur to her that it was unfair or oppressive. They had both merely considered it an inconvenience like all the other rules that adults had for youth.

Olivia was a child, a white girl allowed to go into places that her best friend could not; but she did not feel any luckier or more special than Tree appeared to have felt about herself.

But now she felt her friend's blackness. Rooted, sure, and intimate with the night, folding into dusk like the gray side of a mountain. Strong and viscous, there was depth to this insight. And yet there was something more.

Quick as a flash, Olivia was suddenly in touch with the sideways glances and quick head-up nods that indicated trouble in the advancing form of a light-skinned person. The heaviness of chained feet and the coldness of steel. The caged-up determination and broken-down sassiness. The crushed willingness that stifled anything except the career of survival.

Olivia felt suddenly old and cumbersome, like the weight of a secret much too heavy to keep; and it stunned her to find that this feeling came from the soul of her best friend. It was quick as lightning, come and gone; a powerful blow that might not be named and remembered but certainly would never be lost.

Tree tried hard to feel Olivia, now confident in the magic of the whirling Witchhazel and secure in the potency of sisterhood. She waited for something, anything; but it seemed forever until she heard it.

Her best friend came in a whisper, a sigh that marks the end of a day, a small edge of a thing, hardly noticeable to anyone. Olivia's spirit flew across her best friend's eardrum and down into her throat, light as air. She circled across the heart muscles, twirled within the tight spaces of her mind; and in the blink of an eye the little girl became the hush that follows after a door closes behind you.

Olivia blew in and blew away, disappearing as quickly as she had arrived. Loose and escaped, Tree's friend was merely a breath slipping through fingers.

Witchhazel pulled their heads apart and made a small nick in both of their brows. When blood was drawn she locked their foreheads together and flicked her tongue in a high, shrill voice. Sorrow and freedom mingled and flowed across the minds of the two girls and into and out of the dancing heart of an old woman. Joy and despair began in one thought and ended in another.

Forever, donned in the wrappings of a split second, carried all three of them late into the afternoon. And when Witchhazel, the dancer of dreams, finally opened her eyes, she was alone, standing inside an unbroken circle with the sun lowering into a bow.

A late breeze rustled in the pine needles that lined her yard and brushed across her head bathed in perspiration. She glanced up just beyond her house far from where her tired eyes could take her vision and saw something exceeding her dreams.

The breeze, the needles, the stirring of the dust around her feet, everything in sight moved in rhythm. A perfect cadence of nature playing to the singsong game of two little girls who skipped hand in hand up the path and out of the woods.

Witchhazel turned around to face the setting sun and lifted her chin in defiance to the approaching night.

"Through thick and thin, we more than friends, we sisters!"

The old woman lifted her hands above her head, clapped three times, and laughed.

All living things have names. To be without one is to be lost in a world without definition. What else but a name satisfies forgotten memories, softens the indured layers of a broken heart, brings life to still pictures?

Nothing shall speak too much about a man, save the sound of his name.

—The Color Man

Five

Olivia didn't know that her brother wanted to fly. She didn't know that he ached to sleep or that at thirteen years of age Roy had given up on childhood. She didn't know that the innocence had been stripped in lean watery layers, year after year, because of the things he had learned from their mother's longing and his grandfather's unfisted hand, poverty, and perhaps the consequences of suffering too many regrets.

She knew that he had abandoned his friendship with E. Saul and his Sunday afternoons next door at Ruth's; but she didn't know it was because of what the white boys said about them living in Smoketown. She didn't know that he was ashamed of things he couldn't name and that his heart had closed upon itself.

She didn't know that her brother dreamed of a night woman who untied the red string from around his neck and danced him across the sky, that in that dark place of rest Roy nestled himself in the wings of goodness, that the folding of a day was the only time and place he felt safe.

What she did know about Roy was that he was violent and cruel and that late on a summer afternoon he was christened with a name that handed him the declaration of the man he was destined to be. That if there had ever been a time when he thought of or spoke to her, gently, because of their kinship, a memory she could keep of when he had been kind to her, it was, on that hot August day, like infested wheat in a field, snatched up and burned. That anything good that she would eventually learn of family would come only from what she would be taught from next door.

Just before the day shifted, in the hottest part of the afternoon, the name fell hard on the boy. Harder than the lessons from school that severed his friendship with E. Saul. Harder than staying away from Ruth's porch and not bending toward the laughter and the singing that drifted through his window. Harder than knowing that his mother didn't love him. Harder than stone.

It fell during a game of basketball when the boys had gotten through with chores and farmwork at just about the same time. They gathered at the dirt field behind the old school since they were too young to be over at the blacktop one at the park. The older boys played there and it was a whole different kind of ball game on that court.

Roy and some of the younger kids went sometimes just to watch and dream of the day when they could spit out obscenities and smoke Camels at the same time that they held the ball that fit so snugly in their hands. They longed for their bodies to lengthen, their voices to thicken, and to achieve the grace that the older boys had when they ran from end to end.

Olivia noticed but never commented on how Roy and his friends imitated the older boys, how they laughed, how they pulled and dropped the cigarette from their mouths at the same time, the way they twisted a foot in the dirt to crush out the butt, how they watched and studied the way the older girls looked at the mature boys, all buttery and timid, a far cry from how the younger ones were treated.

Roy had only played a couple of games that summer since Kay Martha had given him work cleaning out the shop and washing out towels. He straightened all the magazines and swept the floor and had kept the job for three summers. He left for good though that summer when he was thirteen and she asked him to hold the curlers while she permed Goldie Creech's hair.

"I ain't no goddam sissy," Olivia had heard him yell when their mother asked him why he quit.

Since he no longer had a place to be or responsibilities to fulfill, Roy got to the playground early that day and threw shots up with Frog Lewis, the boy who always sat next to him in school. Billy Ray and Jake Miller and Tommy Owen came up together an hour or so later, jumping off the back of Mr. Miller's pickup; and before too long they had enough players for two teams. Frog and Billy Ray were the captains and it soon evened out to be the seventh grade versus the eighth.

Like everybody else in town, Olivia already knew how Frog

got his name. He was only six when it happened. His older brother gave it to him because he had a bad habit of sticking out his tongue. So when his mother told him he'd swallow a fly, Thomas called him Frog. The boy didn't seem to mind, however, because at least it granted him attention, something that the name Clayton Henry Lewis never did.

Since Frog wasn't wearing a shirt, his team was the skins and the other three boys wiggled free from their cotton tees to be in correct uniform. Roy took the ball out; and the game that Olivia and Tree watched from the swing set just behind the basketball court started like all the other playground games.

"That's Billy Ray," Olivia told her neighbor as they skipped and pulled themselves up in the air. "He's the meanest boy at the school."

It was a family tradition for the Ray boys to be troublemakers; and Billy, being the youngest, apparently did not want to tarnish what his brothers had made for themselves. He always hung around with Jake Miller and Tommy Owen; and they walked through the halls at school just waiting for a girl to mock or a smaller classmate to bully. Everyone avoided them. The three boys were pimply and angry and spent more time in detention or in the principal's office than they did in class.

Roy thought they were his ticket to the little bit of happiness that he could not seem to find on his own. He believed that if he could just get into that threesome everything would be better for him. So he became their informant, cleverly releasing the names and the paths that were taken home of anyone who spoke ill of them.

He had told them of the closet in the girls locker room that was never opened and bore a significant keyhole and he was the one who stole the science test out of the library two days before it was given. He had even relayed the conversation he overheard between Mrs. Calloway, the math teacher, and Mr. Greeson, the principal, a conversation that prompted a certain amount of vandalism at Mrs. Calloway's house.

The three boys recognized Roy's desire for inclusiveness; but they had not been quite ready to allow someone a year younger to be a fourth partner in their reign at the school. So they baited him for useful information and then they would dismiss him.

Roy was playing a pretty good game, his sister thought, having scored six out of the twelve points his team had. But they were still losing to Billy Ray and the eighth graders, who only had one more basket to get twenty-one. The game had been going on for quite a long time; and they were sweaty and flushed, having played with more than the usual amount of scrapping.

The afternoon was starting to fade and Roy had the ball when Billy Ray said it. He was dribbling, just getting ready to pass it to Monkey Ramos, the boy with the longest arms on the playground, when the name stopped Roy in his tracks and froze the play of the game.

Everyone around, the Bartlett twins who were playing hopscotch next to the road, Davie Ramos, Monkey's younger brother who was standing on top of a mound of dirt playing king of the hill with a few other boys, Olivia and Tree who had stopped swinging and were comparing the sizes of their hands, and Molly Simpson who had just dropped her bike in front of the flagpole, all heard Billy Ray when he said it. It was loud and unmistakable and it fell so hard and fast it stung even the ears of those not watching.

"Do something, Hangman!"

Apparently, Billy Ray had not thought of it before. He had noticed the red ring around the younger boy's neck. Everyone had. But unlike a too-short haircut that called out for names like"Jughead" or "Big Ears," or a new pair of glasses balanced on a nose to be called "Four Eyes," having a sore birthmark clinging to the inside of a collar was almost too frightening to bother with. It was like picking on a child who lost his arm or whose mother had died. There were simply some things that children, even the mean ones, knew were too unkind.

But for Roy Jacobs, the name Hangman fit. It was perfect. Neat and ordered and completely justified. So Billy Ray did not or would not, even if teenage boys could do such a thing, take it back.

When he said it, the name sounded so quickly and deliberately that it stunned Roy, opening himself up to a steal and the winning basket. After that it was over. The surprise in his eyes was all the proof that the boys needed to accept the christening. And all that the sucker punch to Billy Ray did was to write the name in stone.

Frog pulled Billy off of him but only after a string of blows that ripped across the younger boy's face. Roy got up fast and walked away, heading toward the area where his sister was playing, the ballplayers laughing behind him.

When her brother was right beside her, Olivia jumped off the swing. She wasn't sure what she would do, what she could say; but she felt clearly the need to defend him, protect him, comfort him. In spite of how he had treated her in the past, he was family, kin; and he, even to a little sister, was still just a boy.

"Roy," she called out to him, but he didn't stop or glance in her direction. "Roy, wait," she yelled again. "We'll go home with you." And Tree jumped from her swing, landing beside her friend. They started to run, trying to catch up.

The boy immediately turned around and faced the girls. His face was squeezed and tight. "You stay away from me." His voice was low and angry and the white of his eyes flashed. His hands were at his side, balled into fists. Blood pooled in the corner of his mouth.

"You come near me and I'll kill you," he said, louder this time.

And the brother Olivia knew so little about picked up a rock and threw it in their direction. It hit Olivia sharply just above the right elbow. She yanked her arm across her chest, hurt, and grabbed it with her other hand. A bright red swelling immediately appeared.

She lifted her eyes to see her brother pick up another rock. Quickly, she pulled Tree with her and both of them backed away, shocked and frightened at the boy who had just been named.

They turned and ran to the swing set, a few of the children gathering around, while Roy, blasted and wild, dropped the stone and headed into the woods alone.

Although Olivia knew little about her own brother, she knew lots of things about her best friend's sibling, E. Saul. He was the open book she read and they practically knew each other's thoughts. Neither of them slept very well at night; so the girl would often sneak out of the house and find her neighbor in the garden or sitting on the porch.

The first few evenings she came over, he sent her home, telling her that it was too late to be outside, and walked with her back to her front door. After doing that a number of times, however, and especially after she came home bruised from her brother's violent rock throwing, he decided to allow her to stay, letting her fall asleep on his lap while he leaned against the front steps.

Olivia knew that her neighbor wrote long and lovely poems with words and phrases she never understood but that she liked to hear. She knew that he carried seeds in his pockets and that he always kept an eye of worry on his sister Tree, that he thought his mother worked too hard. The little girl knew that her neighbor missed her brother's friendship and that he was troubled at night because of a terrible nightmare.

Unlike Roy, E. Saul found no solace in the hours of darkness. The women in the house thought the young boy stayed up late to read; but the truth was that he did not want to sleep. He fumbled with the night trying to shorten it or disguise it or avoid it, anything to weaken or halt it; but it still always came. And it never came alone. For with it was the terrifying story that played itself across his mind like a moving picture.

In his dream, he told his young neighbor, there were three spiders with threadlike legs and small paunchy bodies, eyes, tiny and black. They hurried along a silver tightrope that wound itself around E. Saul's bed. The one in the middle carried a white milky sack, thrown upon its back, glowing like a bulb. The narrow legs steadied the paunchy body and balanced the sack while the other two spiders led and followed like guards trying to protect the one who ran in the middle.

There was a fourth spider that was stronger and faster than the others. Its legs were long and jointed in the middle, which permitted it a faster gait. It had a hairy body, fatter, with bulging slits for eyes that shifted as it trailed the three smaller spiders that seemed to be running from danger. This one, round and sturdy, crawled along a web that ran perpendicular to the other; and all four spiders met at a corner formed by the lines of silver, dropping into E. Saul's bed.

The three slender spiders stumbled in terror, scurrying across E. Saul's sheets, the sack still balanced across one's back. The fourth spider chased them, first one, then the other, its legs quick and nimble, until it spotted the one with the sack and directed its hunt toward it.

"Here is where I can't decide what to do," he said to Olivia as they sat on the porch, early in the black hours of a summer morning. "I don't know if I should kill all four spiders or just that one that is chasing the others."

He closed his eyes and leaned against the steps, remembering how the spindled spider draped itself across the milky sack and opened its mouth, its large, gaping mouth. "I never know what to do," he confessed to his sister's best friend, both of them hidden in darkness.

Olivia never responded to her neighbor when he told of the dream; she just moved closer to him, dropping her head against his shoulder or nudging herself beneath his arm. They would sit that way for hours until the little girl fell asleep and then he would loosen and fall too; and they would sleep that way the rest of the night until one of them would wake just before morning and hurry them both to their respective beds.

It was how they managed the hot summer nights and the loss and the disappointments they both assumed. It was sweet and harmless and a simple spread of comfort for the two children.

E. Saul found that planting seeds helped with the soreness of the nightmare and the drama he tried so hard to forget. His fingers digging into the cold earth seemed to soothe the festering heart pain as the smooth red clay lifted out the stinging that lay buried beneath the surface of his skin.

He planted flower bulbs, spaced evenly around the walkway, believing that a fortress of tulips and buttercups, hyacinth and iris, lilies and dahlias, would guard his nights and his family by a moat of loveliness that could hold aside troops of evil.

Behind the house was a small patch of garden where vegetables were his defense. Half-runner snap beans curved along a trellis like barbed wire. Straight and crook-necked squash, cucumbers, and sugar babies lay nestled in the vines that lay bridged into the ground, a green and golden impasse. Stalks of sweet corn towered the rear of the fort, a trench dug just beyond. And down at the creek where the soil was wet and fertile he would bury the seeds of fruits and baby the earth that comforted his webbed and troubled mind.

Only in his gardens could he close his eyes without a struggle and lay with his thoughts unshadowed by memories. Sometimes in the late afternoon or the ending hours of morning you would see the young boy asleep with a smile as he lay by the creek or over in Gethsemane surrounded by the sentry of sunflowers.

He was gifted with the soil just as he was with words; and often the two worlds of vision moved into each other so that his poetry was as rich as wet earth and his gardens grew full of stories.

There was perhaps no one who sensed E. Saul's gifts as much as Mrs. Masie Williams, who still bore hard her pain for her son. After Elton's death, everyone tried to pull her away from the other side; but she straddled that place between life and death unable to yield to either world. She talked at great length to voices no one else could hear and mumbled in whispers to the silence that followed her like a shadow.

She could seem just as lucid as rainwater at times and then, right in the middle of an easy conversation about the weather or the price of tobacco, she would stare way behind someone's eyes and tell them to leave her alone and start fighting, yanking at the air.

Nelda was the only child who could tolerate her mother's choice not to choose and the grief that covered her up like skin. She was the only one who stayed with her, the other two children having left long ago. Nelda would sit by her mother's bed late at night, stroking the wrinkles from her brow and cradling her in Bible verses and songs about the Jordan. Mrs. Williams would fold up like a baby and search her daughter's eyes as if there she might find a rope or bridge to pull her completely over. But there was never enough.

Ruth and Miss Nellie thought it was a good idea to share the bounty of E. Saul's talents with the bereaved woman; so at first they would take his flowers and vegetables to Mrs. Williams and later they would send E. Saul or the girls.

And though his neighbor's name had fallen hard, it was only a few weeks later when the season was ripe and hot and flourishing in his gardens that Mrs. Masie Williams, still swallowed up in grief, balanced herself between the two worlds just long enough to anoint E. Saul.

"Well, look here, Mama, E. Saul and the girls have brought us some of beans and corn; and what are these, darling?" Nelda opened the door wide to let the girls and the freshness in.

"It's turtlehead flowers," Tree said, coming up the steps,

Olivia following close behind. "The bloom looks like a face poking out of a shell." E. Saul waited and then walked in with them. "Olivia found them near the creek."

Mrs. Williams was sitting at the kitchen table staring into the rows of jars that lined a shelf near the sink. She did not hear her daughter or pay any attention to their guests or the things they brought them.

Tree walked to her side and placed the flowers near her hands that rested on the table. Olivia moved toward the table and followed the old woman's eyes to the jars. There were pints of green beans and peaches. Then she glanced again at the woman and saw the pure streaks of silver that marked the rows in her hair reminding her of the broken tightropes E. Saul spoke of in his dreams. She turned to see if her neighbor had noticed, but he was standing near the door with Nelda.

"Mama was just telling me how she used to love to hear your grandmother sing. I told her that I didn't know Miss Nellie used to be a singer."

Tree shrugged and turned toward her brother while Nelda shut the door and went over to the sink. She began rinsing off the beans, already planning to snap them for supper.

E. Saul pulled out a chair and sat next to the old woman. Tree and Olivia stood behind him. They saw that the old woman's eyes were small behind her glasses and cloudy. But from left to right they moved following the file of canned vegetables and fruit. Her fingers lifted and fell as if she were counting in her mind and then she stopped and dropped them in her lap. They all watched her without saying a word.

"What's happened to all the colors?" The old woman was speaking to the jars. "There just don't seem to be any colors anymore."

Nelda glanced over at the children, worried that her mother might frighten them. But they remained unchanged.

"Over there behind the catfish pond, Nelda, you remember?"

"Yeah, Mama, I remember." She turned to the sink weary from her mother's memories.

"There used to be the tiniest dandelions over there, like little drops of honey balanced on spare streaks of green." She rubbed her finger and thumb together.

"And the sky, it don't seem to be so blue. Have you noticed that, how the sky ain't so blue?" She faced the visiting boy, stopped and waited for an answer, then went on.

"I remember when the days were nothing but brightness. Strict golden sunlight that melted everything into color. The lines, they were clearer back then, won't no gray. Clear blue sky and the nights were nothing but sheer blackness decorated with pinpoints of white." She punched at the air with her finger. Then she paused, thinking.

"And Easter morning?" She laughed as she remembered. "Now, children, there was the color!" She waved her hand across her face. "Not just nature am I speaking of; I'm talking of the folks who came to church."

Her face became alive. Nelda turned to see the delight that

had poured into her mother's voice. The girls grinned at each other. E. Saul sat silently.

"The men, they would strut down that center aisle at church, oiled up and slicked down and ease into them oak backseats with their crisp brown suits and bright yellow handkerchiefs." She pushed at her hair. "Their shirts were boiled white, then ironed flat and adorned with a tie that would sting your eyes. And they looked good, child. God hisself had to smile at them men celebrating the Resurrection looking so good.

"And the women? Now they weren't about to be outdone by no men." She traced the neckline of her cotton shift. "They'd feed their children dried beans and poke greens for days on end; but neither they nor their children were going to go to church Easter Sunday looking poor.

"All the women, young and old, had one dress that was packed away in brown paper and neatly saved in the bedroom trunk. It lay beneath newsprint or one clean sheet so that there'd be no snags from the lid. And they would wear them dresses to church smelling of cedar and lavender splash, holding themselves tall and proud, 'cause they was fine!"

E. Saul and the girls were entertained, enjoying everything the old woman was remembering. They were thinking about Easter morning and the way they had always participated in the celebration.

"Pink chiffon with pressed silk ribbons. Purple queen lace edged along the seams of a royal crepe skirt. Starched blouses so stiff they rustled beneath their arms and orange velvet hats with a real-live ostrich feather hemmed in at the side. Yessir, then there was some color."

The corners of her mouth dropped and she turned to face the boy sitting closer to her than anyone else had in a long time.

"Just don't seem to be no color no more, E. Saul"—she paused—"except 'round your house." She studied him, hard, like reading a book.

"You sure enough got the colors over there. They fall from your fingers and it's a gift."

She fidgeted with the flowers that lay between her elbows.

"You the Color Man, E. Saul Love; and you got 'bout all the color left 'round here. 'Bout all that's left."

She faced the boy she had now named while one tear fell from her eye and splashed onto the table and split into drops. And for just a brief moment the three children watched as she stood completely on one side.

A bean snapped and she hurried halfway back; and E. Saul, newly named, quickly led the girls out the door and home.

I've got a question
'spect I'll ask the sky
how many deaths do angels die?

There is an answer
maybe time will tell
just make a wish
drop a penny in a well.

I've got a question
guess I'll ask the ground
is everything lost always found?

There is an answer
maybe time will tell
just make a wish
drop a penny in a well.

I've got a question
this one I'll keep
is it best to dream only when I sleep?

There is an answer
maybe time will tell
just make a wish
drop a penny in a well.

—ES, OJ, AND TL
THE JUMP ROPE SONG

Six

"Roy's got another black eye." Tree saw him as he walked up the driveway.

"Hmm." Olivia was busy pressing pine needles into borders to separate the rooms in the square of land they decided to make into a playhouse.

"Who you reckon hit him?"

"I don't know. Do you want your room in front of the kitchen or behind?"

"Behind, I guess. He fights a lot, don't he?" Tree was sweeping the side area with a pine branch thick with green straw attached to the end. She remembered how swiftly and deliberately he had thrown the rock at his sister just a couple of years earlier.

"It means you'll be off by yourself since my room is beside the sitting room." Olivia still had no response regarding Roy; and Tree was having difficulty recognizing the closed door.

She had paid attention long enough to realize that Olivia

would not discuss her mother except in very strange terms. Her friend spoke of her like she was an acquaintance; someone who stopped by to sell you night cream or pass along instructions having to do with hurricanes and voter registration.

She never called her Mother; the thought of which seemed as foreign to Olivia as calling her Daddy or Uncle. There was no apparent connection between the woman and her daughter other than the way one feels connected to someone who lives in the same town or buys the same kind of fabric. That and the uncanny way they both seemed to have in knowing how to forget or put something aside.

There was no malice or ill wishing from the young girl; she was merely indifferent, detached in a way that was cool but not cold, clear but not defined. The way Olivia considered the relationship, it was tidy and manageable. And Tree learned to respect the boundaries that were as real in the mind of Olivia as the pine straw edges that kept room from room in the make-believe house. Tree learned this way of understanding the relationship between Olivia and Mattie over time and without too much difficulty; but she had yet to uncover the lines drawn between brother and sister.

There were other times, Tree remembered, that her neighbor hit his sister—she had seen the marks—threatened his mother—she had heard the yelling. But she did not know the extent of her friend's fear that began first with denial and finally moved to forgetfulness.

She did not realize that for Olivia developing this art of forgetting had become a way to protect herself initially from her mother's lack of mothering and eventually from her brother's fiery demeanor. She did not know that to his sister, Roy was more than just a nuisance like most older boys, he was trouble. Trouble with a violent streak that began to reach much too frequently in her direction. And Tree did not know that Olivia understood that it was dangerous enough that she had to learn to focus on something else or it would consume her. Envelope her.

Tree did not know that Olivia pretended she was an only child. To take Roy out of her life. To get rid of the danger. The little girl from next door, who had violence in her history but not in her memory, did not understand that for her neighbor and friend this tactic was not merely fun and fantasy but rather it had become necessary.

If pushed to remember, Olivia could have told her friend that she had been afraid of Roy since she was a toddler. That even as an infant she felt a harshness from him that pulled her away. She would remember how he always carried her a little too tightly when he moved her from room to room. How there were marks made by his thumbs that left her bruised and tender. The mean and terrible things he would say to her when no one was listening. The smothering feel of the pillow squared in his two hands stretched across her small, white face.

He was cruel and hurtful and had always been. And now that she was old enough to retreat from his tough callused fists and his long virulent stares, it helped if she believed that she did not know him. Slighted the fear somehow. Lessened the sting of reality.

She had fought in self-defense only once. If pushed she could remember that too. Biting with great force into an arm that was intended to wrap around her neck but instead got locked between her teeth. Meant to choke her because of something she had said. She couldn't remember what. She drew blood but she also took a beating when she finally let go. She was rescued by a blow across the boy's back, hard and low, given by some drunken bedmate of Mattie's.

Olivia suffered very sore ribs, more than likely broken, and a crook in what used to be a short, narrow nose. She was bloody and rent and she never tried to defend herself again, knowing that counting on a mother's lover was like counting on Santa Claus; and that was a luxury that only the very foolish or the very rich could afford. Instead she stayed away from Roy and tried to make him into someone else's sibling.

"What you suppose make boys fight?" Tree was still very interested in her neighbor's injury.

Olivia was through making the pine straw borders that divided up the house into rooms and was deciding what to build next. "They just boys."

She stood up to admire her architecture. She was proud of the straight lines and the spacious living areas she had designed. She loved the thought of her own house, hers and Tree's, that was sure to be void of violence and drunkenness.

Here was the house she dreamed of. And there were no chambers for fear or loneliness, no closets to hide in and lock, no doors to stand behind. This house was complete with joy and friendship, built in just as carefully as studs and joist. Walls were light and dressed in photographs of a neat and happy family.

Corners were innocent and free of crouching children. Floorboards bore no stains of neglect. The kitchen was warm with smells of hospitality and kindness. Bedrooms were filled with a rich silence that spoke of deep and restful sleep. The windows faced the rising and setting sun that reached over mountains of lovely flowers and fields of green and golden earth. Here was the home that freed Olivia from the boarded-up life she tried to live. Here, in a make-believe house that could be shifted by the wind, a house of straw and wishes, here in this place was the longing of her heart.

"Maybe it's that stick in their pants." She walked over to Tree who laughed and fell into the sitting room marked by stones.

"Well, it could be." Olivia replaced the marker that had been kicked into the kitchen. "I seen Jerry Hanslow messing with his. Maybe it hurts." She thought about the consequences of having a twig in her panties and found her idea quite believable.

"Maybe it rubs against their legs and starts a sore. Maybe that makes them irritable and they pick fights with other boys because seeing them reminds them of the raw spot between their legs." She knelt down to work, satisfied with her theory on violence in males.

Tree rounded out the border in the back and drew four squares around a circle. "Do you think that's what made my daddy hit my mother?" She sat in one of the squares, considering Olivia's idea. Maybe her friend was right, she thought. Maybe it was just as simple as having an extra body part, a flap of skin that hangs at the meeting of their thighs.

Olivia stood up and dusted off her hands. "I don't know." She paused, remembering the story that E. Saul had told the two girls one evening when Tree had asked if he remembered their father.

E. Saul had told what he knew quickly and carefully, saying only that Mr. Love was a man of troubled spirits, a man who liked to see children and women cower at his arrival.

"But what did he look like?" Tree had asked her brother at the time, as if having a picture in her mind, knowing his features, would grant some image to the absent place in her memories.

"I don't remember," E. Saul had said. "And it doesn't matter anyway."

But it did matter, at least to Tree. And she had told this only to her best friend, understanding that for her family a discussion of Mr. Love was then and would always be forbidden.

Unlike Olivia, who did not seem curious about the man who was her father, Tree found herself searching for the one everyone called Ticker. Not literally, of course. She and Olivia both knew that their fathers were dead. They had heard Mattie tell Ruth that Olivia's father had drowned in the Mississippi River and early one Sunday morning they had wandered down by the grove of sunflowers and at the back of the church to see the small gray stone that stood scratched and unleveled in the puddle of weeds. They knew Tree's father lay inside the earth, face and body decomposing in the dirt.

And yet, while Olivia seemed to find comfort in her ignorance, acted as if the untold story was a relief, Tree wanted an image, an understanding so she tried to make up the features of her father using the composites of men she watched.

"I know what he looked like," Tree said to her friend as they built their make-believe house.

Olivia stopped what she was doing to listen. She knew that Tree had been trying to find her father a long time.

"He's got eyes like Mr. Matthews, you know dark, set deep in his head."

Olivia thought about the man who stood at the crossroads near Smoketown every morning, waiting for somebody to give him work. The quick way he winked and then turned in another direction as if he were searching all the time for the right truck to round the corner and come in his direction.

"He was tall like Bishop Clover, that man who comes every year to preach revival at the church. I think my daddy was built like him, long-armed and hard across his chest." Tree pulled her legs close to her, thinking how right she was, how right was her picture of her father.

"I think he had a wide smile with full, steady lips, that he was light-skinned, more like E. Saul than me."

Olivia listened, considering her friend's description, wondering how long she had been breathing life into a dead fallen shadow, how long she had been giving image to the man who apparently had left only deep and narrow cracks in the hearts of those who remembered him, who knew how he really looked.

"I think he didn't talk much and that he walked real fast, that he combed his hair flat to one side, a part made deep to the right, that he rolled his tongue on the outside of a pop bottle like Old Man Smith, and that he dipped his chin when he spoke."

The little girl stopped. She realized that she could not think of ugliness or of her father's horrors when she imagined him, that she could not focus on his misgivings even though she knew some of his sins. One that he ran out on her mother and her brother and the other that he always came back expecting more than what was his. And yet, these trespasses did not blight the form she conjured up of the man she never called Daddy.

"I know everything about him," she confided to her best friend. "I can hear his voice. I can see his back and his sturdy neck. I can call it all into being, see him like it was really him, waiting on me, coming to find me. I can see it all." She hesitated. Olivia waited.

"Except for his hands. No matter how hard I try, I can't call up a picture of his hands."

Olivia noticed the winding path to the front door of the newly constructed home and considered whether to rim it with flowers or pieces of brick. She figured that she could find something in the field or out by the driveway; but she decided not to leave Tree just yet. She sat down and thought about what her best friend was saying.

How had Tree's father's hands looked? she wondered. Were

they thick and leathery, unfeeling from the wasted years of clutching thorns and hoe handles? Were his fingers long and cold? His palms, were they smooth? His nails square and short or ragged and dirty? Did he outline the cheek oh so tenderly before he slapped it openhanded? Did he hide his fist down beside his hip, gripping and releasing before he swung it? Were his knuckles darker than the skin above and below? Were his hands big enough to wrap around a woman's neck with the same ease they wrapped around her waist when he twirled her to fast music or held her to himself during the slow, easy songs? Were they quick and nimble like a doctor's or clumsy and misdirected?

Olivia understood that her best friend, who bore no intimate information of violence, who could not recall the feel of fist on cheek or remember a strangling hold around her throat, that a mind like hers, a mind so unspoiled and innocent, would not be able to conjure up evil in the form of a man's hands. She knew that her best friend had never worn and therefore did not know the markings of a violent man's most personal weapons. And no matter how long she searched, no matter how often she peeked down the arms of men, white and black, until she understood the consequences of angry hands, until she felt the blows across her face or back, she would not be able to make herself imagine evil in the form of fingers.

Just then Roy rounded the corner and stomped toward the porch. He leered at his sister who quickly fell out of his way, holding up his hand like he was going to hit her. Roy lowered his fist and stretched open his fingers. Olivia turned quickly toward her friend and in that swift moment before the punch landed Tree yelled.

The boy turned in her direction, scowled, and walked away. Olivia shook her head and looked back at the path she was building while Tree, not knowing what just happened, thought she heard a rock fall and land somewhere near her heart.

I've got a question
'spect I'll ask the sky
how many deaths do angels die?

Miss Nellie was watching out the back window when her young neighbor came behind her with that question. She was enjoying the ease with which two children can build a family. The simplicity of all of life when watched from a window that opened into the pretend world of little girls. Even if one is black and the other is white. She was so caught up in the silliness and the strength of their play that she did not notice that one of the girls had walked up to her kitchen door and had said something. Something about Mrs. Williams. She couldn't make out the first part of what they child said, but she did hear the question.

"How come you don't sing no more, Miss Nellie?" Olivia had come through the door. "Somebody said you used to sing."

It was a simple question really. It wouldn't take a lot of thought to answer her. She didn't even have to answer. She could just brush her out the door as if she were interrupting some important task. She could have sent her back to her play. She was a child after all; and children didn't have to be answered.

Or if she wanted to give her something, she could just say because she was too old. Or too tired. Or just didn't enjoy it anymore. Anything would work because all those things were true. But they were not the truth. And Miss Nellie understood the difference.

Even tucked away so far behind her heart that she could actually enjoy the picture of her granddaughter playing with a little white girl, she knew the truth was still alive inside of her.

Nellie Star Broadnax could always sing. It was more natural than talking for the youngest child of Virginia and John Smith Broadnax. She was born years after the war but in a place in South Carolina where freedom had not been properly introduced. So Nellie Star started out in the fields like all the other black children. Chopping weeds and pulling cotton until Big Missus discovered the tiny girl's sweet and tender voice. Then she was taken out of the field and into the backyard to sit by the old woman's window to sing.

Big Missus was suffering from cancer that tore away the chords of her voice and left her choking on the walls of her throat. The old woman found that the voice of the slave girl calmed her, soothed the tangled ropes that burned and chafed her need for words. So just as old King Saul used the youth and sugar of David to temper the fever of demons, the Big Missus ordered Nellie to sing and soothe the passage of her breath.

Nellie did not like her new task though it kept her from the painful bend and yank work that the others endured. She loved to sing and liked the cool of the breezes that shifted through branches near her head. But while her parents plowed and picked cotton and her brothers broke horses and chopped wood, Nellie sat on a milking stool under a window singing, hating herself and her privileged gift that left her mouth and spirit dry and her fingers restless.

Big Missus wanted her available at all hours so Nellie slept in the woodshed near the big house and away from her family and the other slaves. She was set apart, different; and during all those nights when she peeked around toward the quarters and heard the low talk and smelled the late fires, she longed to give away her gift and gradually learned how to be alone.

Singing was not the only favor Nellie Star had. There was the matter of a knowingness that gave her extra insight. She could predict things like the change of weather and when a bout of trouble was coming and how it was shaped. Virginia believed that her daughter was blessed with an angel and that she must learn how to pay attention because angels did not waste themselves on those who did not hear. And then her mother taught the little girl how to listen, not with her ears, but with the curve of her neck, down along the base of her spine and beyond the nerve endings that spread across her back like a road map.

She could tilt her head and follow the delicate push of gossamer wings and know the direction of someone's sorrow. She would close her eyes, touch the breeze with the tips of her fingers, and follow the shift of tomorrow's pain.

During the long hours when Big Missus didn't want singing, Nellie Star learned the codes of a messenger angel that spoke of heaviness and gave hints about how to help others run for freedom they already had but didn't know.

The angel would give her a glimpse of certainty on the nights when the water's tide was low enough for crossing and the regulators were busy at other farms. And when the glimpse became a vision she would begin to sing. Her voice was light and velvet; and as her volume grew those who had been planning to run would know to pad their shoes.

They would understand just by the teasing tone of the little girl's song to run toward the mouth of the Savannah River. Here they knew from passing slave talk that it broke through the foothills like an open wound and dropped into the French Broad River that eventually splashed onto the lips of the hard-to-reach mountains. Away from the long rows of cotton. Away from the never-ending tobacco fields. Away from the whip-torn mounds of flesh and the forever rumble of stomachs that didn't have enough to eat. Here, they believed, since they had heard no contradictions, was where they would find their liberty.

Now the angel, of course, did not reveal all things to Nellie. She was not told, for instance, what had already passed. And that they were all free to go as they wanted, not needing the light and tender voice of a little girl sitting on a milking stool soothing the throat of an old white woman. Nellie never saw the icy death lurking in the frigid winds that wrapped around the mountains facing the end of a river. The angel did not show her the poisonous fangs of the brown water moccasin that swam just below the surface of muddy water. There was no glimpse of the wild dogs or the nimble bobcats that fought for the caves and ate flesh.

There was just enough to convince the child and the other slaves that the angel was truly on their side. And that required little or no evidence since each of them hungered for any news that God had not deserted them. So it wasn't until much later when the bearded man from the North came riding up with the news everyone else had heard that she learned of the cold mountain deaths of hundreds of South Carolina slaves and first began to doubt the angel's blessedness.

After the arrival of the bearded man who spoke of freedom, she and her parents moved to North Carolina where they were sharecroppers, a new way of describing the old slavery. And she continued to sing though not for any Big Missus. Nellie Star became very popular in the riverbank gatherings and the little cabin churches that flourished along the now broken South. And the young gentle-voiced girl grew into a tall straight-back woman with a voice that saved souls and melted hearts.

One such heart was that of a skinny young man who brought her candies and told her stories of Africa. He was wiry with soft eyes and a smile that sneaked from his eyes down across his lips. He was smart, could read, and knew about things that Nellie Star had never dreamed of. He told her about the war and the split in white people's minds. He knew about the North and places black people could work and make decent money, own their own homes. He wrote poetry that she turned into songs; and together they were the music for tenant farmers and Jesus-loving poor folks.

She had little need of the angel during those few years, so she quit listening. Besides, she had always felt a certain burden for having such a gifted responsibility; and she was glad not to need it anymore. Now she trusted in the foreverness of love and believed in the promises of a brilliant young man who dropped chocolates in her lap.

She married Robert Blackwell on a sunny day when the wedding music was just loud enough to cover up the whispers of a loose-lipped angel talking of death. And eighteen months later she did not see the glint of a silver blade in the hand of an angry drunk man as it ripped apart the flesh that clothed her lover's heart. She did not hear the pounding of her name in his brain that soon quieted to a footstep. She did not see, did not hear, did not understand until it was too late.

When the rumbling of the angel finally woke her, she left her baby girl sleeping and raced to the place she had seen in a dream. But by the time she arrived Robert was dead and the pounding had ceased.

She did not curse the angel this time, however. She even continued to sing, though a bit of her magic was gone. No,

Nellie Star did not splinter and break until she felt the tightening around her neck and discovered that God gives out nothing for free.

John Smith Broadnax was too old for picking cotton; but he wasn't too old to defend the home he built and paid for. So when the two white men rode up and shook the dirt off their boots onto his porch and went in without knocking, he grabbed his shotgun with the reflexes of a boy and fought them both with the strength of a man years younger than himself.

The white men were surprised by his agility but welcomed the struggle and found that they enjoyed whipping and hanging an old man who reminded them of their youth and emphasized their power.

Virginia died stretching toward her husband, kicked and gun-whipped in the head without a thought as they pulled her husband to the nearest tree. She too spoke Nellie's name, but it did not speed the flight of an unsure angel.

Nellie was folding laundry, watching Ruth dance, arms outstretched in a sliver of late afternoon sun. She was even humming a song for dancing when she felt the heavy brush of smoldering wings.

Nellie walked first, then ran, praying to the belligerent angel. Begging her not to tease. Speaking to her like a dutiful child speaks to a parent. Begging forgiveness for not believing. She talked to the angel like a friend, calling her names of affection and promising her things like faithfulness and adoration. But when she got to the tree and saw the dream was too late, she cut down her father, washed the fatal wounds of her mother, cursed the angel to hell, and never sang again.

Olivia was stunned by the silence and the grievous glance that peeled from behind the old woman's eyes. Her choice not to sing had nothing to do with time or age or even forgotten melodies. It took only one look at her and she knew Nellie Star did not sing because something or someone stole away her song.

The little girl did not wait for an answer. Even at her young age, Olivia had learned enough about the lives of old people that she understood there were some things she did not need to hear.

She walked out the door, returning to her play with Tree, and simply left her oldest neighbor standing at the window, a truth too heavy to speak.

I've got a question
guess I'll ask the ground
is everything lost always found?

School started late the year Tree found out about her parents. The rains were delayed, the days long and hot; and because of that, the tobacco fields couldn't be harvested until deep into the month of August. Since both communities, white and black, were dependent upon the crop for their livelihood and dependent upon children for help, the school year began and ended at the discretion of farmers and the whim of southern seasons.

Glorietta Pope was the one who wrote and passed the note during math lessons to Tree, a note that everyone read and waited for the little girl's reaction. She sent it from the rear of the classroom all the way to the front seat where Tree was sitting. Mrs. Little had left the room to see about getting someone to help her open the windows while the class was supposed to be working on their multiplication tables.

Tree was on the eights when the small torn and folded piece of paper was slipped beneath her elbow by Terrance Walker, the new boy in school who sat behind her. The note was on the bottom of a homework sheet, the sentence written in large black letters penned by the hand of a ten-year-old: "Your mama killed your daddy."

Tree folded up the note and stuck it in the side pocket of her new pair of pants as the teacher walked into the room with the janitor, Mr. Glass. The little girl didn't even glance around to see who had sent it. She turned the page of her math book and moved onto her column of nines.

When the day at school was over, she spoke to no one, not even her brother. Instead, she headed straight for home. Olivia was already there waiting to discuss her teacher's means of discipline and a boy who had started fourth grade at the age of fifteen. But before she could begin to tell her stories or ask her best friend questions about her class, Tree walked up the steps of the porch and into the house, put down her books, and turned around and walked out, heading in the direction of town.

"Hey, Tree, wait!" Olivia had jumped up and was following her. "Where you going?"

The little girl never answered. And the two of them walked in silence past the empty field where the church had burned, out beyond the row of houses on the main road, the drugstore and the tobacco market, and down the curve to the house where Ruth worked as a cook and a maid.

She went to the kitchen in the back and knocked on the door. Olivia followed closely.

Ruth heard the knock and was soon standing at the door.

"Lord, child, you walk by yourselves all this way?" She glanced up the road to see if there was anyone else with them.

Olivia smiled. "Hey, Miss Ruth."

"Hello, baby. You have a good day at school?"

Olivia nodded.

Ruth stood at the top of the porch. The girls were perched on a middle step, one behind the other.

"What's the matter, sweet girl?" She shut the door and walked down to her daughter.

"You kill Daddy?"

Olivia slipped down a step, one foot falling over the other. The question made her dizzy.

"What, child?" Ruth steadied herself against the banister after making sure her neighbor was okay.

"I asked you if you killed my daddy?" Tree moved closer to Ruth.

"Where did you hear that?" her mother asked, her voice having turned soft and wobbly.

"Doesn't matter where I heard it. Is is true?" The little girl suddenly sounded old to her mother, old and troubled, like a woman in need of help.

Ruth paused, opened the door, and went inside. After a few minutes she came out with three glasses on a silver tray. Olivia took one look at the grand display of refreshment and thought it was the most handsome thing she had ever seen. She took one of the glasses from her neighbor and drank down a big swallow of lemonade.

Ruth balanced the tray on the edge of the banister and took one of the glasses herself. She held it out to her daughter. Tree did not reach for it. She did not budge. She waited for her mother to respond.

The older woman set the tray on a step and pulled a dark blue handkerchief from her apron and wiped her face. She was tired, Olivia could tell; and the woman stuck the rag in her pocket, sat down, and slid over to make room for her daughter to sit beside her.

Olivia sat on the ground next to them. She was anxious to hear Ruth's reply and she wondered how Tree had kept such a question to herself for the entire walk from Smoketown. She wondered how her friend had managed to wrap up and hold her pain.

Ruth took a long swallow and then set the glass on the tray. She peered around the house to see up the street, thinking about her employer and how much time she should take to tell her daughter her story. Tree sat with her gaze focused directly on her mother. Her chest rose and fell with each hard breath.

"The first time I went dancing with your daddy, he said my

eyes were strong and carried a light breeze in them that made him think of the ocean."

The little girl had heard that her parents met at a softball game, introduced to each other by a cousin they shared. She didn't know that it was the slow dance at the Little River Delight juke-joint that blistered them, heart by heart.

"There were royal blue lanterns hung about the place, torn and dusty; and the smoke wrapped around us like a wall. The music was thick and dreamy and somehow it dragged us into each other while drawing us into itself." Ruth grew quiet remembering how their bodies pushed and pulled against the weight of the song until finally they relaxed and fell into the arms and neck, the chest and hips of the other.

He leaned into her with the sound that named him. "Tick, tick, tick." He whispered in her ear the clicking voice of tongue against roof and felt her grow and melt into him. And from dance to table talk, from dusk to morning, from juke-joint to riverbank they lost themselves completely.

"I fell in love with him," Ruth said to her daughter. "With his dreams." She glanced at her side and noticed that Tree had softened a bit. She handed her the other glass and Tree took it.

"I fell in love with the sound of his tongue and the way he could sing."

Olivia smiled.

"I think he fell in love with my innocence, the way I wanted to believe everything he said."

Ruth paused thinking how they were the carriages for each other and long in coming; so that when they married they did so without any hesitations nor did they entertain doubts since they both believed so strongly in the vigor of that first dance.

They lived in the silent house with Miss Nellie since they had no other home. And though the old woman was never rude, Ruth knew that her mother did not trust the man her daughter loved. There was too much hunger, she had told Ruth, in the way he dreamed and planned. Too much desperation for the slow ways of the world. Too much intensity for a black man.

Ruth understood now that Nellie knew that hunger in the spirit never goes away. That it may be slighted or cooled or may take another form. But it is never completely filled so that she was not surprised when a hole tore between them.

"I did the same work I do now. I cleaned the houses of mill workers." Ruth thought about how hard it was to find work in those days and how she walked three miles to the village and cleaned from eight until six, then she walked back home and cleaned her own. She made almost two dollars a week, which was good steady pay. And now with the new thought of love keeping her company, she walked a little lighter and was not dampened by the long hours.

"Your daddy, Ticker," she said his name as if Tree might not recognize it, "was a necklace of dreams strung together by my determination to love him." Ruth leaned against the door.

"His first dream was to own his own farm. Build a house for his wife and family and sell crops in the same line as white farmers. He figured that he would be the envy of all the sharecroppers because the land he worked would be his own; him, the only boss."

Ruth, in the beginning, had loved the idea and understood when he told her he could not work while he was dreaming because there were too many things to do. She understood how hard it was trying to find just the right piece of land. And she explained to Nellie how much negotiation it took for a black man to get a fair price. She did not mind when Ticker dipped in the savings or took her check to spend time at the pool hall because she understood that this was where the best deals were made.

"Then it wasn't long before Ticker quit dreaming of farming and talked about moving north. He filled my mind with thoughts of long red dresses and nights of big bands and felt hats."

She took another swallow of lemonade, recalling how she had never thought of moving and was a little unsure of leaving her home; but how she became just as excited as he when he told her stories of railroad cars and buses that took them downtown. So that when he danced with her and clicked his tongue in her ear, she did not pause before she emptied the money jar and gave it to him so that he could try to win a poker game for tickets.

"That was the first time he hit me," she said to the two girls. "And at the time, I thought he had the right, that it was just a part of the price for dreaming."

Tree dipped the glass to her lips, wondering how close she had come in the imaging of her father.

"The next time it was panning for gold in California; and it took fourteen dollars to buy the right equipment. I packed my bags this time and waited for a signal; but that time he hit me with his belt buckle." She reached up and touched a small scar that was right above her left eye. "I stopped the bleeding in my forehead, quietly put away my things, and did not think again of gold."

The two girls listened as the woman talked about how her marriage became a cycle of dream and violence, how she believed his apologies with the same enthusiasm that she believed his ideas, how little by little her mother's silence grew thin.

Ruth set her glass down on the tray, wiped her mouth with the back of her hand. She set both hands beside her, steadying herself as she laid out the family history to her daughter. She was nothing but truth. She told the story exactly as she remembered it, exactly as it unfolded along the edge of Smoketown.

"When I became pregnant with your brother, Ticker got a job. He worked loading bales of cotton; and for a few months I thought things were better, that the way we lived together, the beatings he gave, had been broken by the dream of our new baby. But when he quit his job and drove to West Virginia with that shine in his eyes, I knew it was not the shine of our baby."

Tree rested her head against the railing, listening, her breathing slowed.

"This time, however, he made bigger plans and moved me and Mama to the house we live in now. Only then we had to share it with another woman and three children. It was dirty, like you never seen before." She peered down the road at a group of white children walking to their homes. "But he told us it was only for a little while and left us to go back to West Virginia with a friend."

Ruth paused, remembering how he missed the birth of his son but returned with gifts, sweet wine, and the promise that he would come again for them. He told stories of fast promotions and how well he was liked so that when Ruth questioned the plan and complained of rats he was angered by her mistrust.

"He blamed Mama when I asked him how long we had to live where we were and he hit her across the face." She turned to her daughter, making sure she was still able to hear what was being told, making sure that she should keep going, that she shouldn't just finish and set the story down.

Tree had dropped her eyes away from her mother.

"I should have done something then," she said, nodding her head. "I should have stopped things right then." She made a humming sound deep in her throat.

Olivia slid her finger across the top of her glass. The rim was smooth and edged in gold.

Ruth continued. "Your grandmother and I cleaned and rebuilt and planted and painted and we didn't mind at all when the other woman and her three children moved away. It felt like a home again; and we were all happy." She stopped and smiled. "And then he came back, and this time without no dream."

Ruth hesitated and then decided not to tell her daughter how for five years she and Nellie protected E. Saul and struggled with the dreamless man, how she learned to hold her breath without drowning while he forced himself upon her and stole away her hope. She recalled but chose not to explain how she was able to close herself off to the blows across her body and make herself the wall that locked away her mother and her son and pretended it did not hurt to stand so still.

And since she thought her daughter was too young and did not need to know everything she did not tell her that Ticker took the company of other women. Drunks and addicts mostly, that he even brought some of them to their home, took them in their own bed.

"The women in the neighborhood, they were good to me those years," she said to her daughter. "They brought me ice packs and poultices." Ruth paused again, remembering the way she was cared for, the way the women came around, easy and unrequested, how they mothered her through the bad times. She remembered how they never interfered or offered her a place to stay until she was six months pregnant and bleeding from her eyes.

"Your father was aiming for the side of my head because I think he enjoyed watching my neck flinch and the way I'd get when I was scared, a way that usually made me turn away." A breeze stirred in the wide arms of the trees beside where they sat. The rustle of leaves surprised them.

"But this time, I don't know why." She turned to her daughter and lifted her chin, cupping it in her hands. The older woman smiled. "Maybe it was because it was you inside of me." Tree waited.

"But this time," she said again, "I stared straight at him. I wasn't afraid; and the tip of his belt flew up into my eye, cutting it from top to bottom."

She dropped her hand from Tree's face and slid it down the front of her dress.

"I think he was stunned by how I looked, by how my eye split and bled. I don't know what it was, but I know he was surprised by something because he threw down the belt and walked away. It was as if he suddenly couldn't hit me any more."

Ruth stopped again; because here she knew it was tricky. Here, she knew was what her daughter came searching for; but to tell it, to say it out loud, was a hard and unusual thing to do.

"I don't know who put the gun beneath the porch steps," Ruth said, her voice suddenly clear and bold.

She paused, remembering that the secrecy was part of the success of the women's lottery, a means of punishment used only in extreme circumstances in Smoketown.

She learned later that the detailer was the one chosen by the selection of the ink-dipped straw drawn out of a coffee can in the back of Sadie Coble's woodshed. That this person simply made the necessary arrangements; the decision to carry out the plan made by the detailer was always clearly only one woman's to make.

Ruth also knew but didn't tell her daughter that the gun was Maurice Coble's and had been resting in the shed near the can. It was cleaned and loaded and returned so quickly Maurice never knew it was missing. The detailer had the responsibility of securing the weapon.

Later one of the women told Ruth that everyone appreciated the fact that the detailer, whoever she was, stood by her word and took care to find an easy gun for a woman to handle.

"I was surprised, I think," Ruth confessed to the two little girls, "by how the gun felt when I dropped down to pick up some tomatoes that had spilled from my bag."

Ruth remembered the early morning, the red vegetables tumbling through the wet, torn paper bag, the sun sliding across the porch, the shock of finding the weapon so neatly hidden, the coolness of the barrels.

"But something happened to me there with my belly dipping low beneath my legs. And I stood there, completely calm, sliding my fingers up and down the shaft and along the trigger."

Olivia and Tree were quiet and wide-eyed. They waited for the final part of the story that they both knew had to be on the way.

"At the time, I did not lift it or even pull it out to look at it. I just sat there on the ground feeling the wood and the steel." The older woman glanced out across the street, watching the sun falling behind the trees and knowing that she still had at least an hour's worth of work to finish.

"Three days later when your father raised his hand and peered behind me and noticed our only son, your brother, E. Saul, and then looked at me like he had finally figured out a way to make me hate him for good, I did not hesitate one minute."

She stood up behind her daughter, stretched her back, with both of her hands sliding down her hips. "Not one minute," she repeated.

The color of the sky was as orange as Olivia had ever remembered seeing it and the little girl turned first to see the sun and then to the front of the house where she noticed a boy peeking at them from behind a curtain. She turned around to Ruth to hear the rest of her neighbor's confession. Tree was facing the road in front of her, but Olivia could see that she had closed her eyes.

"I took the gun and pulled the trigger one time." She stopped and smoothed down the front of her apron-covered dress. "Just one time."

The little girl flinched as if she heard the shot.

"So, yes, child, I killed your father. The law treated it as self-defense, did not arrest or charge me, but call it what you want, it remains as it was. I killed him."

The two girls were as still as wood.

"And if my life was to play itself over, same people in it, same streaks of meanness even from the man I love, the man who could take a common afternoon and turn it into magic, I'd do it again."

The older woman bent down and picked up the three glasses, placed them on the tray, and started to walk up the steps.

"I'm sorry, child, that you had to be brought into this world like that, that the man whose blood runs in your veins had such a twisted mind. But I suppose it's good that you know the truth. I suppose it's always best to know the truth."

She peered down at her daughter and paused as if she might say something more; but she just opened the door wide, and walked inside.

Olivia and Tree got up from their seats on the steps of the back porch of the house where Ruth cleaned and cooked, afternoon shadows falling around them like misbehaving ghosts, and without a word between them, headed home.

I've got a question
this one I'll keep
is it best to dream only when I sleep?

In the beginning, Olivia could tell that her mother pretended not to notice the changes. Not in her appetite. Not in the way dresses draped where they used to cling. Not in the way she could never get enough sleep. It seemed to her daughter that Mattie closed her eyes to the gray and ghostly image that stared back at her from the mirror and made herself believe that she was the twenty-something girl who could turn heads and open wallets with half a smile and the cut of her eyes.

Olivia imagined that her mother pretended it was envy that she saw in women when they walked by the house, granting no possibility to the notion that it was nothing but simple pity that made them shake their heads and move to the other side of the street. And she did not seem to notice the deplorable dismissal from the men when they rode by, the men who used to pay, pretending instead that they turned her away when she called to them from the front porch because she was too rich for their poor blood. Olivia figured that Mattie made herself believe that she could still make a man beg and truly thought she was desirable.

It seemed to the little girl that this pretense was the only way Mattie would get out of bed and go to the toilet, open the window, or choke down a piece of toast. Mattie's game of make-believe was beggarly, even to a ten-year-old, but Olivia understood that if her mother couldn't pretend, she could not survive. And even though the little girl could tell her mother was wasting away from disease and denial, that survival itself was primarily a fantasy, Mattie's daughter would continue to do whatever it took to keep the woman alive.

It was not because of anticipatory grief or even the fear of being an orphan that kept the little girl pushing and pulling her mother away from dying. That would have made more of the relationship than what there was. No, Olivia didn't want her mother to die because she knew that without the presence of a mother, even a poor and sick one, she would be left to the care of strangers in thick black suits who carried briefcases with mounds of paperwork and who always assumed they knew what was best for children.

Olivia had seen these people before. A couple, a man and a woman, both acting like they cared for the little girl and her brother, came sniffing around their house when Mattie was arrested and put in jail. She was drinking a lot those days, and she had apparently gotten mad at some old lover and thrown a beer bottle at him. Billy Ray told Roy how they had to wrestle his mama to the ground, she was so mad. "Like a bull," the teenager told her brother.

Olivia had overheard the two boys talking just before the social services personnel had come to their house asking questions about how many days the two children had missed at school, what they had for supper, and if Olivia had ever stayed by herself at night. When her mother returned later that evening, the child walked Mattie to the bedroom, helped her undress, fixed her a bowl of butter and syrup, and vowed never to let strangers, especially those in dark wool suits with brown folders in their hands, in her house again.

When Mattie got worse, Olivia, with the help of Ruth and Miss Nellie, nursed and cared for her. Even though her neighbors begged her to go to a doctor, her mother refused and Olivia was relieved. She was, after all, worried that if someone discovered how sick Mattie was, the man who wrote down everything she said and the woman who smiled just a little too much would return, forcing her to leave their little home at the edge of Smoketown. And Olivia, though certainly not rich or safe, could not fathom a life beyond the one she had.

Finally, after Mattie took to the bed for good, having become unable to pay her rent, Kay Martha, concerned and frustrated, came by to collect. Her former employee was three months late with the rent; and the landlord was beginning to feel as if the young woman was taking advantage of her. She didn't know that Mattie had gotten ill; she had only heard the gossip about the drinking and had seen the police reports that were printed in the local paper.

It was Saturday, late in October, and the day was surprisingly warm for the passing autumn season. She walked from her shop, after closing early, and discovered that the sun was more intense than she had anticipated. She was dressed for a church revival service that was held later in the evening, a dark velvet dress with a long silk ribbon tied behind her waist. Her stockings clung to her legs while drops of sweat began to fall along her forehead, forming a tiny row of beads just at the band of her new red felt hat. She moved slowly at first and then sped up, wishing that she had waited until the following morning to make such a long and ambitious journey.

The landlord arrived at the front door, knocked first, and then peeked in the window. She saw no movement in the house that she had made possible for the Jacobs family; and she stood for a few minutes, waiting and listening. She was about to leave the porch and head home, leaving a notice in the screen door, when Olivia came around the corner, holding a scrawny yellow kitten.

"Hey, Miss Kay." The girl smiled, surprised to see a visitor. Olivia liked the woman at the beauty salon where her mother used to work. She had always been cordial to the Jacobs children.

"Hello, Olivia." The woman in a hat and velvet dress remained standing at the front door. Olivia walked up the steps to join her. "Who you got there?" she asked, pulling at her dress that was sticking between her legs.

"Oh, this is Butter," the little girl answered, thinking that the woman was terribly overdressed for such a simple Saturday afternoon. "Me and Tree found her in a storm drain at the feed store." She held the cat out to Kay Martha.

The woman reached out and scratched the animal behind its ears. A drop of sweat fell from the side of her head. "Hmm," she made a humming noise as if she had discovered something unexpected. "It appears it needs something to eat."

"Yeah, I was just going to get it some milk." She walked past the woman to the door. "You want to come in?" Olivia opened the door and held it with her elbow. She was not considering the consequences of bringing her mother's former boss into their home.

Kay Martha walked in behind her, curious and unsure. The house was cold and dark, not at all a reflection of the afternoon sun, and she was glad for the shade and for a cool room. She turned toward her left and noticed that the door to the main bedroom was closed.

She hadn't seen Mattie in a number of weeks. A few months earlier, just at the end of summer, the young woman had started missing days at work and then, a couple of weeks later, she just finally quit showing up. Kay Martha had come by before but had never found anyone at home.

"Your mama here?" The woman glanced around.

Olivia put the kitten down and retrieved a can of milk that was on a shelf above the kitchen table. She found a saucer in the sink and poured a bit of the old milk into it and set it on the floor.

Kay Martha peered into the kitchen. Most of the shelves

were empty and dirty dishes were stacked on top of the stove and counters. She waited for the little girl to answer.

"Mama is gone to town," Olivia replied, rubbing the kitten as it drank the milk. She didn't look at the woman since she was nervous about telling a lie.

"Oh," Kay Martha responded, glancing toward the rear of the house where she was sure she heard a rustling noise.

"She had to run some errands," she added. Olivia noticed the woman's focus. She heard her mother stirring and the little girl stood up and moved to the doorway. "That's our dog. He must just be waking up."

Kay Martha nodded. "You have a dog and now a cat?" she asked, having no memory of the Jacobs family bringing a pet in the house. She knew that Mattie never liked animals.

Olivia bit her bottom lip and turned in the direction of her mother's room. "Yes, mam. It's a big dog too. I suppose you might not want to see it." She was hoping now that the woman she had invited in would leave.

"I don't mind big dogs," Kay Martha replied suspiciously, her hat now cocked to one side. "Is he in the bedroom?" The woman started through the door, moving past the child.

Olivia jumped in front of her. "I don't think you want to go in there," she said, her voice suddenly loud and nervous. "He's sometimes real mean."

Kay Martha could tell that the little girl was trying to keep her from entering the rear of the house; and she hesitated, considering that there could be something terribly wrong and that maybe she should check on things. She had been worried about Mattie since she quit coming to work and wasn't sure if she was just staying drunk or if she was sick and in need of assistance.

Kay Martha paused, however, before she kept moving and noticed that there was a look about the little girl, a sort of desperation in her eyes, the need to keep her mother from being seen. She didn't know if it was shame or fear that kept the little girl so guarded; but the woman dressed for evening worship didn't go any further. She decided to honor the walls the child was building.

She studied Olivia and saw the signs of frailty, of a loose recklessness, and decided that she didn't need the rent payment anyway. She hadn't seen the boy, Roy, in a long time; so she didn't know of his condition. She didn't even know if he was still in the home, though there were signs of a teenage boy evident throughout the house.

Before she left she waffled in her decision to leave things alone in the Jacobs house. She considered that Olivia would be turned over to the state and would get better care in a government facility than she did in that little house, that Mattie would be better off too. But the flash in the young girl's eyes, the apparent need to hold on to her mother, and an obviously deep attachment to a neighbor child kept Kay Martha from changing her mind. She assumed the woman next door, the one who helped her deliver Olivia, was taking care of them anyway, so she finally became clear that she would not intervene.

"Okay, Olivia." She cleared her throat. "I won't check on

your big dog." She straightened her hat and stuck the notice of past due payments in her purse that hung at her elbow.

"Just tell your mother that I stopped by and if you need me, if she needs me, you come by the shop and find me."

"Yes, mam, I will." Olivia walked the woman to the door and held it open.

Kay Martha stopped and turned toward Mattie's room and then again to the little girl. She sighed and then walked out the door. Olivia stood watching as the woman headed up the street toward town. Then she closed the door and went into her mother's room.

Mattie, lost and unaware, did not recognize the goodness of a friend. She didn't know of the debts that her former boss and landlord paid. She wouldn't know that Kay Martha began buying the family groceries and paying their bills.

She breathed. She took in. She let out. But beyond that, she was void. She had long since lost her role as mother. Since the bonds had been so flimsy from the beginning, it was not difficult to believe that she had become detached. Just as she had managed not to see the rest of her reality, she pretended not to see the son who grew more violent as his body changed from a boy's to a man's.

She turned away when he leaned into the other child, throwing aside the memories of her own father's heavy hand and angry temper. She tugged the pillow over her head to silence the blows that she knew the younger girl was taking. And as the pretending grew more and more difficult, Mattie slept.

It was a dreamless sleep and fretful, filled with the tossing and turning of undecided hope, marked by the too-deep wounds of life. The disease just below the surface of Mattie's flesh was nothing compared to the temptation to forget larger and larger pieces of her life. So that as the cancer of her memory grew, gaps in her life widened and began to pull her down with a force greater than the multiplication of irregular cells, more destructive than forgetfulness, and without the mercy of time.

Mattie, unable or unwilling to comprehend, was, however, visited by snatches of tenderness even though she could not remember the faces or the names. Kindness changed her sheets and soothed her sores. The small childlike hands of her daughter would pull a blanket to her chin, brush her hair, feed her fingerfuls of jelly, and spoons of sweet milk. Mattie would lightly stroke the hands that cared for her, trying to call out a name, trying to capture the angel. But bit by bit, little by little, Mattie began to die.

Her daughter's vigilance, however, the one pair of tender hands that visited her, pulling her up and through hour upon hour, kept death at bay. Time and time again, night and day, minute after minute, as the woman pleaded for her passing to come, one child willed it not to be so, her determination so fierce it pumped life through Mattie's veins.

For even though Mattie could not remember her children, tried not to remember her childhood, she seemed to be left with one maternal instinct, one solid place to land her sights on mothering. Somewhere winding through her chaotic thoughts and beating reluctantly in her brain, she knew.

If she died the youngest child would be left with nothing

of family except for the son of a jungle orphan who wrapped anger and mistrust so tightly within himself that it bled through the skin of his neck.

So Mattie, who was not even aware of the power of motherhood, completely without a picture to recognize or compare it to and who was desperate to die, clung to the tiny bits of life that slid down her throat tasting like ripe strawberries and began to measure her dreamy, nightmarish state of living spoonful by spoonful. And only and all because there was a tiny, ragged thread of memory and hope unevenly rolled together and stitched loosely to a corner of her heart, and only because her daughter refused to let her go, Mattie did not die.

April 4, 1943

Mr. Roy Jacobs
317 Pinetops Road
Greensboro, NC

Dear Mr. Jacobs:

We are sorry to inform you, but you did not pass your physical for orientation into military service. The physician reports that you suffer from hypertension and therefore would be unable to carry out the responsibilities required of a soldier.

We thank you for your interest in being a part of the nation's finest and hope that you are able to find a position that best suits your needs.

Sincerely,
Sergeant Thomas B. Clearstone
United States Army
Fort Bragg, NC

Seven

Olivia found out from Jeanie Maddox, Billy Ray's girlfriend, that Roy was sixteen when he got laid for the first time. "Billy put him up to it," the teenager reported after she saw Roy's sister sitting on the sidewalk. She stopped to talk. "It was his idea in the first place to leave home."

Jeanie had come into town to shop with her mother who was still in the fabric store studying patterns. Olivia was sitting near the flower store on Main Street. She was resting after having left her house early that morning hoping to sell some rags.

The young girl started ripping up bedsheets from her house and old towels that she got from Kay Martha's beauty shop when she found out that she could make a penny a cloth. She even collected them from her neighbors and from folks in Smoketown and then she sold them to the butcher and to Mr. Henry, the man who ran the general store near the curve in the street.

She was sitting on the sidewalk, counting coins, when the

older girl walked out of the store and stood next to her. Olivia slid over, giving Billy Ray's girlfriend plenty of room.

"You know, Hangman," then she stopped a second, then said his real name, "Roy, went to Fayetteville to sign up for the army." Jeanie dropped down beside Olivia. She smelled of hay and sweet grass. Olivia thought she was lovely.

The young girl nodded, unsure if Jeanie was asking it or telling it. But Olivia had already figured out what had happened to her brother when she opened the letter that had come for him, postmarked from Fort Bragg. It had been sitting on the kitchen table for three weeks when she finally decided that Roy wasn't coming home. She was curious about what a fort had to say to him.

When she read that her brother hadn't been accepted into the army, she worried that he would soon be back. It had been a couple of months since she had opened the letter and she was just hopeful enough that maybe he had found something else to keep him away from Smoketown.

"Billy and Tommy were set on being in the army." Jeanie eased into a sitting position and then rolled her eyes. "So they were the ones who talked Roy into joining them."

Since Roy quit school earlier in the year, Billy Ray and Tommy only had to convince him to leave Tootsie's Billiards where he worked afternoons. They came by the day before they were going to leave, Tommy's seventeenth birthday, and asked him to join them. Which he did. Without too much hesitation.

"They had filled out all the papers, had their physicals, and were supposed to talk with a sergeant the next day." It was all pretty routine, a simple procedure since the military was still in need of fresh soldiers to replace the ones who were coming home from the war.

"I went with them." The older girl leaned over and held up some of the rags from Olivia's bag. She set them down and slid her feet out in front of her.

It was late in the spring and Olivia noticed that Jeanie had on new sandals. She studied her own shoes and was embarrassed that she was still wearing boots, big, brown boots that she got from a neighbor of Tree's, a boy neighbor. She pulled her feet behind her.

The teenager continued. "You know, so I could be with Billy his last night as a civilian." She winked at the younger girl.

"Candy wasn't a bad-looking woman," Jeanie reported as if the young girl knew who she was talking about. "For a whore, I mean." She elbowed Olivia.

The young girl folded the top of the paper bag and held it tightly in her hands. It seemed a bit uncomfortable to the eleven-year-old to be discussing her brother's virginity right out in the open like they were. She glanced around to see if anyone else was listening.

"We hitchhiked all the way to Fayetteville and found a bar on the edge of town that didn't care whether or not we were eighteen." The teenager began twisting her hair. She was pulling long strands and then wrapping them around her finger.

"We got drunk on beer and shots of Wild Turkey and later Billy decided that Roy needed to get laid before he went off to war." She stopped playing in her hair and started to fiddle with the hem of her skirt. She rolled it under twice, pulling it above her knees.

"That's when we met Miss Candy." She drew out the name, making each syllable long and interesting. She grinned at Olivia.

"She had on a store-bought purple dress that was too small for her and was wearing some strappy black high-heel shoes." Jeanie had memorized the woman completely.

"Her hair was curly and yellow; and the old cow was painted up like Christmas to cover old acne scars." She leaned against the side of the building where they were sitting. "And she had on fake eyelashes and too much lipstick."

She straightened up. "A fine time," Jeanie said the whore had yelled when they were walking down the street, "is what you boys need."

They ended up following the woman as she headed around the corner from the bar, down along a side street, through a couple of alleys, and up the fire escape stairs of a building facing the slave auction block that sat in the middle of town. There, they all went into an apartment where the rooms were divided by thin curtains, darkness, and a thick wall of smoke. Candy motioned Billy Ray and Jeanie into one room and Tommy and some other girl into another and then, holding Roy's hand, headed into another section of the apartment at the front of the building.

Jeanie told Olivia that when she came out of the room to get something to drink, Roy was sitting uncomfortably in a straight-back chair watching Candy undress in front of him.

"I saw the whole thing," she said to Olivia. She smiled, then laughed as she sat next to Roy's little sister, remembering how awkward the boy had appeared.

Candy knelt in front of him, pushed his legs around her, touched his face, her fingers melting into his skin. "This your first time, ain't it?" she had asked as she pressed her thumbs along the bones of his cheeks and the curve of his jawline. She kissed the lids of his eyes and called him, "Baby." As she moved her hands near his throat, near the scar around his neck, he quickly pulled her hands into his and pushed them down.

Then she began to unbutton his shirt and undo his belt. She smiled when he fumbled with her clothes. And she took his hand and guided his fingers across her. She whispered in his ear. And she rolled beneath him like the earth in a dream. When it was done, when he was done, she squeezed him tightly, moved from underneath him, kissed her finger, touched his lips, got up from the mattress on which they had lain, and walked into the darkness.

"It was sweet," Jeanie said, deciding not to share any of the details she had witnessed with the girl.

Olivia blushed. It embarrassed her to know someone else had been watching Roy during such intimacy.

"When we woke up, the two women who had been with Tommy and Hang . . . I mean Roy, were gone." Jeanie smoothed her hair down and raised her chest and shoulders, tightening the top of her blouse and showing off her figure.

"Then they all went over to sign up." Jeanie pulled out a pack of gum from the pocket of her blouse. She held it out to Olivia who took a stick. The older girl opened one and began chewing.

"That's when Roy found out he didn't get in." She saw some other teenage girls across the street and waved at them and then turned to the little girl who was trying to unwrap her gum.

"And you haven't heard from him?" she asked, surprised that someone in his family wouldn't know where he was.

Olivia shook her head. She stuffed the stick of cinnamon gum in her mouth. It was hot and sugary.

Jeanie sighed. "Billy said that he overheard everything in the sergeant's office." She turned to Olivia and hesitated. Then she decided to go on. "He said that the guy started the interview by asking Roy the same questions he had asked him and Tommy."

She crossed her legs at the ankles and spread her hands out on her thighs. She studied her nails. Olivia noticed that they were short and round and pink.

"But," she added, "Billy said that the sergeant seemed mad at Roy even before he asked him anything."

Olivia set the paper bag beside her and with interest waited for the teenager to explain.

"He said that the man wanted to know why Roy quit school and what he was doing."

Olivia thought about her brother's job and wondered if working at a pool hall was disapproved of by the military.

"Then he wanted to know who his daddy was." Jeanie

seemed ashamed to say this to Roy's sister. She knew that Olivia's mother was not married to either of her children's fathers.

Olivia turned her head away from the other girl. Her face felt red.

"Billy was filling out some other forms while Roy was in the sergeant's office," Jeanie explained, "and he told me that after the man asked Roy about his father, that then he asked him how old he was and whether or not he had gotten fucked the night before."

Billy shook his head when he was telling his girlfriend this part and Jeanie figured that Billy felt sorry for his friend and that he told her about the interview because he felt somewhat responsible for what happened. She didn't say these things to Roy's sister.

"The sergeant had then asked Roy what he had planned to do in the army. Billy and Tommy had both said that they wanted to fight in combat; but for some reason, Roy had told the sergeant that he wanted to fly."

Olivia did not respond. She didn't know what her brother had meant and yet she could tell it had been a bad thing for him to say.

"That made the man laugh," Billy reported to Jeanie before she left for home and he left for boot camp. And they both understood that at that point the interview really went sour.

"Fly?" the sergeant asked. "Where you think you are, boy? This ain't no fly station. Did you see the sign when you came on base?"

Apparently, Billy told Jeanie, Roy didn't answer.

"I said, did you see the sign when you came on base?" the man asked again.

This time, Billy said that Roy spoke up. "Yes," he replied.

"And what did it say?" the sergeant asked.

"United States Army," Roy answered.

Then Billy said that the sergeant kept on hammering him. "You think you can fly in the United States Army, boy?"

Roy hesitated and then finally responded, "I don't know."

Billy said then that the man seemed to go for blood. That he was loud enough that everybody around the office heard him.

The teenager recited word for word what the man had yelled. "Well, you ought to know," he shouted. "A soldier don't fly, boy. A soldier marches and crawls and slides on his belly. There ain't no flying in the army, boy, unless you plan on moving dead men from one place to another. That what you planning on doing, moving dead men?"

There had been no reply this time, Billy said.

The sergeant kept on. "Then I expect you better pay attention before you stand in line or sign your name on something."

Then Billy said he asked Roy if his mama knew that he was there and that Roy hadn't answered.

After that Billy was told to finish his forms in another office and he never saw his friend come out of the interview. He just knew he didn't get in. He had met up with Tommy and Jeanie later at the bar where they had been the night before and reported what went on.

Jeanie didn't repeat all of the story she had heard from her boyfriend. She had not intended even to tell as much as she had to Roy's baby sister. She thought that the little girl might have known some of what had happened; but she could tell by the blank expression on her face that Roy had not been in touch with anyone in his family.

"What happened to Billy?" Olivia asked, wondering how long the couple had been away from each other.

"He stayed in Fayetteville for a while." Suddenly the pitch of the teenager's voice lowered. "Then they sent him to Germany." She took in a breath and let it out slowly.

"I haven't heard from him in over a month." She pulled the gum out of her mouth in one long, narrow rope. Then she twirled it around her tongue and stuck it back in her mouth.

"I hear that all the soldiers fall in love with French women," she said, sounding sad to the young girl.

"Oh, well." She jumped up, shaking her head. She saw her mother coming out of the store down the street. "Tell Roy to stop by if he comes home." She patted Olivia on the head.

Olivia nodded and pulled her bag closer.

And then as the older teenager walked away, flipping her hair with her outstretched fingers, Olivia sat on the edge of the sidewalk and imagined what must have happened to her brother.

She wondered if he was denied entrance into the military because someone had heard of how he had treated his sister. She wondered if they didn't let him in because they knew that he was mean and cruel or if it was the scar around his neck.

She wondered if he had fallen in love with the whore whose name was all sweetness or if he was on his way home again.

She stood up, grabbing the bag and stuffing it under her

arm, and walked across the street to the feed store, hoping to make a sale.

❧ ❧ ❧

April 10, 1945
Mr. Edward Saul Love
319 Pinetops Road
Greensboro, NC

Dear Mr. Love:

We are happy to extend to you an invitation to study with us in Greensboro at the Agricultural and Technical Training School. We are confident that you will enjoy your education at this campus and look forward to having you as a part of our student body.

You will be receiving other information soon regarding the status of your scholarship and loan applications as well as registration and housing details. Please fill out and return the enclosed acceptance form so that we can retain your student status as a freshman for Fall 1945.

All best wishes as you finish out your high school education and again, congratulations.

Respectfully submitted,
Mr. Earl T. Jones
Director of Admissions

E. Saul's acceptance letters into several colleges made up for all the lost things in Miss Nellie's and Ruth's lives. He was the pearl of a great price, the treasure hidden in the field. And it was worth all that they had struggled against, fought for, and dreamed about just to see him start to fly. He was the son who could take them out and away from everything Smoketown had stolen. He was the new world, the new South, the new black man. And they delighted in his accomplishments, his test scores, his scholarships as if each one was a step bringing them closer to heaven.

Since before he even started school, the two women had begun packing their dreams on his shoulders, feeding him their aspirations, and measuring him for the costumes of their desire. Even with the problems they had with his father, even with trying to live with a violent and bitter man, they still managed to nurture what they were sure could grow in the soul of a little boy.

When he responded by reading at the age of four and solving math problems before he started first grade, they knew he was their ticket out of misery, out of sadness, out of being poor women, even out of being black. He was the song of salvation they sang every time they bowed to pray.

Early in the morning as he sat at the table making rhymes and calling out words he could spell, they pulled out their abandoned passions and slipped them easily under his tongue. Deep in the afternoon when he napped under the tree, they carefully brought out their neglected hopes and pillowed them beneath his neck. And late at night on those occasions when he would sleep, they took down old wishes and blew off the dust, balancing them ever so gently across his back.

They nurtured him on all the things they had locked up and put away and it gave them immeasurable joy just to think of all that the little boy could do, all the things he could give them, all the places he would carry them.

It wasn't long before the dream wasn't just Ruth's or Miss Nellie's. It became more than just the hopes of a prejudiced mother and a biased grandmother. It became more than just somebody else's little boy. Everybody in Smoketown started to think that E. Saul was of their own making, birthed of their own withered hearts; and they congratulated themselves that they had been a part of creating such a smart and dutiful boy.

Teachers sent home notes about his abilities, detailing how he had answered the difficult problems they had manufactured or how he had written papers or solutions that they had inspired. Preachers and principals commented on which choices he should make with his education, proudly expecting him to follow in their footsteps and go to the schools they had attended. Neighbors asked to hear him read his research reports, trying to find anything to which they could lay claim, a story, a memory, a beautiful phrase. Everybody in Smoketown wanted to think they had a piece of the bright young man who knew words like they knew sorrow and could pull color from a rock.

"I used to take E. Saul fishing," Tincan Gentry would say when he heard that E. Saul had won a history contest as if somehow the moments spent on a quiet riverbank had taught him how to store up names and dates.

"I showed him how to pull a string across a row before he plowed it," John Cotton would add as if this had given the boy his brilliance.

"I slipped him his first seed," one neighbor would say proudly, like this had granted him his ability to do math.

"Me, his first paper," another would brag, like it had been the one paper that caused him to understand how to piece his own words together.

And Ruth and Miss Nellie would smile and invite them in, letting them share in the joy they all felt about E. Saul Love. They were, after all, not stingy with their pride.

Olivia had been the only one who thought to ask E. Saul what he wanted to do, whether he wanted to be president or go to law school, whether he was going to study literature or medicine. Everybody else around him was already so busy making the plans for his life, making him into their own dream images, that no one had thought to find out what he wanted to do, which ambitions were really his.

She asked him on a Thursday, the day before he graduated, as she sat on his front porch waiting for Tree to walk home from school. The semester was quickly coming to an end and so far the young man had not made a commitment to any school or profession.

It had taken him completely by surprise that someone had wanted to know, that someone had really wanted to know, that someone was giving him the question without already planning to tell him in the next breath what it was they thought he should do, where they thought he should go to school, or where it is that they would have gone if they could have.

It had been his young friend, his sister's best friend, who had no other expectation or dream to hoist upon his shoulders, no other fantasy for him to fulfill, who had honestly wanted to know, who had asked the question and grown silent without leaving him a look of longing that made him answer untruthfully. And so, the day before he was going to be honored as the valedictorian of Greensboro Second School for the year 1945, the day before he received the Principal's Award for the Year's Best Student, the day before his mother spent six weeks' pay on a party to celebrate his bright beginning of adulthood, he sat down next to his young neighbor and told her what he had not told anyone else before.

The afternoon opened before them like the clear spring sky, wide with possibilities.

"I want to farm." It was just as simple as that.

Olivia, who was leaning on her elbows, her head tilted up, her eyes closed, fell toward him in disbelief. She immediately glanced around, wondering if Ruth or Miss Nellie were anywhere close and had heard the startling news of a boy who would be their king. When she realized that no one else was at home, no family member other than the young man, she stared in shock at her best friend's brother, the smartest boy she had ever known, her tutor and teacher, the one all the other children came to with their homework.

She faced him, showing some sign of surprise.

E. Saul continued without noticing the reaction of his little sister's friend. He was savoring the chance to be candid.

"I'd like to buy that piece of land behind the church and plant corn, maybe soybeans, then maybe switch off one year and grow tobacco. I'd like to have a tractor and three barns, a couple of horses and mules, maybe some cows."

Even though he had never said these things out loud, it was obvious to the young girl that E. Saul had thought all of this through. She tried to monitor her surprise. She dropped her head and listened.

E. Saul rested against the porch railing beside her, his brow eased, his eyes distant. He was enjoying the sound of being honest.

"I'd like to change this house, maybe stretch the front a bit closer to the road." He reached out and gripped a railing. "Maybe add a little fence all around it, put on a new roof."

Olivia thought about the leaks in his house, about how many times she had helped empty the buckets with E. Saul and Tree.

"I'd maybe hire some of the neighborhood kids to help me, you know, give them something constructive to do, run a small business, sell the produce in town or maybe drive to Raleigh to the market." He had considered all the details of his dream.

"In the winter I'd do the carpentry work on the house and barns, paint or plaster; and in the summer I'd never go inside until the moon was halfway across the sky."

Olivia turned to see her neighbor's face, the brightness in

his eyes, the uncensored pleasure in finally being able to name what lay beneath the silence.

A breeze stirred around them and the two of them stopped talking to hear the soft sounds of the season, the singing of a lone sparrow, the flutter of the leaves on the sweet gum tree that stood tall and full in the left corner of the yard.

"What about college?" Olivia asked in hesitation, already measuring the weight of the question, already sad for those women she loved like family, those women who did not yet know the burden of this disappointment.

He turned to his sister's best friend and immediately began to answer the way he had answered everyone in the past three years about where he was going to go after he graduated.

He started to say, "I'm still considering my options," which were the words everybody else in Smoketown loved to hear, words that sent a chill of delight down their spines, words that pulled up on the corners of their lips and could not keep them from grinning since never before had they known a black man who had options, since never before had they even imagined what that could possibly feel like. That's what he started to say to her and then he paused and realized the sincerity in her question, the loose and easy way she meant it.

"I don't know," he answered uncomfortably.

Olivia nodded. She knew that E. Saul had been accepted at five or six colleges, a couple of them somewhere up north. She knew because every time he got a letter from an admissions office, Ruth had thrown a party. Catfish, pork chops, banana cream pie, the menu was endless. She stewed beef and fried fish until everybody was having trouble sleeping at night because they were eating so much more than they had ever eaten before. Ruth was spoiling the community in her pleasure, having already managed a special supper at least once a week for the past two or three months.

When he heard from the school in Atlanta, an acceptance notice that was hand-delivered by some man at the college who was also promising him tuition and living expenses, Ruth had cooked so much food that the next day they were still wrapping it up and giving it to everybody who walked by.

In his mother's mind, E. Saul was getting out of Smoketown and in his departure he was automatically paving a way for the rest of them to join him. First his little sister who would go to the same college and then his mother and grandmother who would live near them and lovingly help them raise their children.

E. Saul had not thought of a way to explain his decision to his mother who so desperately wanted to leave her life.

"What about your writing?" Olivia asked. She saved every poem he had ever given her and some she had taken from his pad of paper without him knowing.

"Who says a farmer can't be a writer?" he answered. And to hear him say it, it made perfect sense.

"Don't you want to go to school? Get out of here?" Even though she was white, Olivia was just like everyone else in Smoketown. She too was trying to figure her way out. She and Tree had already planned to leave together.

E. Saul shrugged his shoulders. He liked school, liked to

learn; but he loved the earth more, loved to dig his hands in the dirt, watch things grow. He knew an education would offer him more opportunities, give him more space to make a life; but the truth was, he really didn't want to go anywhere else.

He liked Smoketown, liked the history and the familiarity of the place, liked the coolness of spring and the crisp chill of fall. He liked the way the soil could hold water and the way the narrow creeks flowed straight into the beds of three rivers.

He was not naïve. He knew the consequences of racism that everyone around him had suffered. He knew how hard it had been, how hard it still was for a black man to make anything of himself in the South. He knew that if he chose to stay at home and farm, like all the other men in Smoketown, that he would never win the approval of the white people in Greensboro, the respect of town leaders and officials. And he knew that's what everybody else in his community, everybody swollen up with pride, was waiting for.

But the truth was, E. Saul understood that he would never win that anyway. He knew what the other people in Smoketown didn't know, a diploma or certificate might help you get a good job or help you make a path into the city, but it would never change the minds of white people. He knew because he had seen how they leered at him when he entered and won the regional spelling bees and speech contests. He saw the sting of surprise in their eyes, their looks of disgust that a black boy had beaten their perfect white children, and he realized then that being smart, winning awards, having perfect scores did not change what white people saw when they looked at him.

His mother hadn't seen it because she was blinded by her pride, so hindered by her desires. She had thought she was watching respect and honor when her son received his trophy or plaque at the hands of a white man; but E. Saul had recognized the disdain. He understood at a very early age that white people might have to give a black person what it was that they deserved; but they never had to give it with approval.

Unlike what Ruth and Miss Nellie thought, E. Saul understood that he would always and forever be black and no matter what a college said you should call him, he would always and forever be judged by the color of his skin.

"What you going to tell Ms. Ruth?" Olivia asked, honestly pained by what she knew would destroy her best friend's mother.

"I guess I'm going to tell her that I'm going to college somewhere close by." He seemed disappointed.

"I guess I'm going to tell her that I still haven't decided what I want to do with my life." He blew out a breath of air.

"I guess I'll wait until I graduate from a university and then tell her that all I really want in my life is to make things grow, that my dream is the same dream her father had, the same dream his father had, and his father before him."

He glanced out across the long golden fields that surrounded their houses and thought of all the backs and shoulders of the men he stood upon. All the longings and dreams and desires that could be summed up so easily, so tightly.

"I want to be a farmer, own a little piece of land. I want to add color to a world that sees only black and white. I want to laugh with old friends and read books and fall in love. I want to be left alone and drive a truck on a dirt road and not be afraid. I want to dream my own dreams instead of having somebody else stuff theirs inside me. I want to see my mother smile and not because I passed some test or won some award. I want to see her smile because she knows I'm happy, not special or gifted or the best, but just because she knows I'm happy."

Olivia watched as the young man shifted under the weight of such a heavy load. She knew he was not quite finished with the answer to her question. She waited as he angled his body in such a way that the sun pressed itself hard upon his already encumbered shoulders.

He stared into the endless sky and completed what he wanted to say. "I guess I will wait four more years and hope that she has found her own dream or at the very least somebody else to waste hers on; and I will tell her what I have known for a very long time. I will tell her that I want to come home." He sighed, concluding the speech he had practiced for years.

Olivia dropped her eyes away from the favored son that she, like everyone else she knew, admired and adored, and watched as the sun slid behind a cloud embarrassed that a boy could be so burdened on the day before becoming a man.

NELLIE STAR BROADNAX BLACKWELL

NOVEMBER 13, 1868–MAY 5, 1945

Nellie Star Broadnax Blackwell of 319 Pinetops Road died Monday, May 5, 1945, at her home.

The funeral will be held at 2:00 P.M. Friday at The Ashley Grove Church, AME Zion Congregation, by Reverend James Irvine.

A native of South Carolina, she has lived most of her adult life in Greensboro.

She is survived by her daughter, Ruth Blackwell Love, and two grandchildren, Edward Saul and Teresa. She was preceded in death by her parents, three brothers, and her husband, Robert Blackwell.

She was a loving mother and grandmother, a good friend. She will be missed by all.

Eight

Everybody knows that bad things come in threes. But when Miss Nellie died only one person saw it as the beginning of the evil that was to unwind its way around the two little houses on the edge of Smoketown. Only one woman knew it for what it was but she had already resigned herself to her own passing and had no way to send along her knowledge. No one else knew to start at the place of Miss Nellie's death and say to a gathering of believers, "Let us ready ourselves for the coming of the devil."

No one painted blood along the entrance of their doors or hung crosses on their bedposts. No one burned sage or splashed holy water. No one held a vigil in preparation, fasted and prayed or lit candles. No one opened their eyes and saw what was so clearly happening in front of them because they were all blinded by a brief afternoon of uncontained self-indulgence, lost in a few hours of bliss.

They missed the omen because of the grandness of the celebration when it happened. They failed to pay attention to their better judgment because of the seductive nature of encumbered joy and the numbing of the senses as a result of having been so satisfied. They resisted what they normally would have seen so clearly because everyone had only and always relied on the dead woman for warning, and they just didn't think that her final counsel would come as violently as death.

E. Saul's graduation party held at the house just at the corner of Smoketown was the Kingdom of God banquet that had never before or would never again be enjoyed by folks living or dead. It was the dinner where nobody walked away hungry, nobody left wondering how something else might have tasted, no one headed home thinking of another meal.

Ruth and Miss Nellie had been planning the dinner for most of the boy's life; so when the evening finally came, there was not a serving spoon unused, not a dish unprepared, not a dining wish left unfulfilled. Fingers smacking, toes tapping, it was the wedding feast only Jesus could have imagined.

There was meat from every sort of animal the residents of Smoketown had ever milked or slaughtered. Long, narrow cuts of beef, marinated in a sauce that caused even the preacher's wife to lick her thumbs without apology. Pork ribs steeped in dark honey, chicken fried in new grease, even goat meat and lamb stewed until the pieces fell off the bone, delicate like the swing of loose leaves in autumn.

There were tender collard greens with thick strips of bacon, fresh green beans and yellow squash stirred with curls of sweet onion, pickled beets and cucumbers soaked in vinegar, pinto beans with chow chow, and potatoes cooked every way conceived, baked, fried, browned, mashed, and cut up in neat little cubes and mixed into salad.

There were big juicy beefsteak tomatoes that nobody, not even E. Saul, could figure out how Ruth had picked so ripe when it was so early in the season, and piles of bread and saucers of butter, roasted ears of silver queen corn, and buckets of barbecue slaw.

There were so many desserts that they were placed in another room, a church table spread across a feather bed. There were fruit pies and cobblers, peach and gooseberry, rhubarb and ladyfinger apples, white and chocolate glazed cakes, sugar cookies and butter mints, plate after plate of sweetness.

The amount and display of food were endless and people were so full at the final hour of eating, they lay down in bunches, rested and gratified in a way they had hardly deemed possible on earth, some of them sleeping as soundly as they did when they were babies wrapped up tight in feed sacks and slipped inside a dresser drawer.

There was nothing missing, nothing forgotten, nothing left uncooked, anything and everything planned and carried out, all the way down to the tubs of lemonade and spiced tea that were set in the middle of the front porch. It was all as it should have been. So that even though Miss Nellie rocked before she fell and held out two fingers before she dropped, the senses and capabilities of everyone in Smoketown, everyone present at the honored boy's party, were dulled and slow.

Nobody recognized trouble in a place where such perfect

joy had been unloosed. And nobody thought anything other than what a shame that death would happen in the midst of pure pleasure since it was clearly the best party anyone had ever attended. And they did not consider anything of a vexing nature since Miss Nellie, now dead, was the only one in the community who had ever recognized the early shades of malevolence.

Ruth's mother was, after all, the one with the gift for catching sight of trouble. She was the one who smelled the coming of evil. She heard its faint whisper of arrival. So without her to warn the people with the interpretation of her dying, without her to contradict what the deacon reported, that she wanted to die in the center of splendor, they simply gathered her up and laid her in the arms of death. They wept and read Scripture, prayed and sang crossing Jordan songs; but they did not look upon her dying as a means of the beginning of anything worse than an old woman who passed over after just having tasted a bit of glory.

They paid no attention to the fact that she collapsed while Mr. Eden, the school principal, was speaking about how he thought it might be time for representation from the community on the city council and how he thought Edward Saul might just be the first black man to do it. No one noticed that she had the attack at exactly the moment when the preacher was walking out the door, having blessed the boy, his path, and the deep but hidden desires of his spirit.

They did not see that her heart stopped beating when her young granddaughter and the little white girl came up together, the young neighbor acting like kin, reaching up and wiping off a tiny bit of strawberry syrup smeared just on the right corner of the old mother's completed smile, that the woman had fallen and died after nibbling on a fruit pie that finally had used all the sugar in the house and was baked in a borrowed dish that was blue crystal wrapped in a tiny red ring.

No one present put the puzzle pieces of prophecy together or heard the loose tongues of angels until it was too late. No one made the connection between denial and death, pleasure and pain, fate and consequence, until everything had come and gone. The three faces of evil: silence, hatred, and ignorance, merging and intertwining like the start and finish of the Trinity.

Even Ruth did not notice the timing of Miss Nellie's demise. More than any of her company, she too was caught up in the delight, too blinded by the joy of seeing her one true dream come to pass. She was so filled up with the mounds of food and the delicious looks of appreciation on the faces of her friends that she did not recognize her mother's choice of death. She was so mesmerized by her pride and the bursting love and the congratulations of the entire community that she refused to pay attention to anything but loveliness.

She did not see the twitches of her mother's mouth as if she was needing to speak. The lone tear that ran from her right eye. The pitch-black stare toward heaven and angels that never seem to come on time. Even the child who knew her mother as if they shared one heart, one spirit, did not see the lifting of the dying woman's hand as a means of trying to stop the coming of pain. The coming of pain that was so unspeakable, so unbearable that she would rather die than say its name.

Later, as the weeks passed, after she shook off the afternoon of feasting, Ruth still did not see her mother's death as a sign because then there was something else blocking her vision. Then she had to fight with the unexpectedness of loss. The grief was like a thick wool veil that dropped heavy before her eyes. She was blind to her mother's message because at first all that she could see was the satisfaction of a full and righteous dinner and next a life without the woman who had nursed her through every crisis, every shadow, every white-heated day.

After she got finished with the grandness of the banquet that she and her mother had pondered for more than a decade and worked for months to bring about, she could not make herself consider anything more than how she could get along without Miss Nellie. The bereaved daughter could not concentrate on what it all could possibly mean, the lone tear, the unspoken words, the two-fingered cry for help, because she could think of nothing except the tearing in her own spirit.

Ruth had never considered the possibility that her mother would one day die and especially that she would die on that one day. Her presence at the beginning and ending of every morning and night, her hand steadied on Ruth's shoulder, her sideways glance of approval, the private and generous talks at midnight, the sharing of this now come and gone dream, they had all become a given in Ruth's life; and now what was given had been taken. It threw her long and hard.

After the party and during the time of death Ruth moved

through her mother's funeral and beyond, like her next-door neighbor moved through years. She was a woman darting in and darting out, watching glimmers of recovery and turning away; but that was all.

She did not think, did not feel, did not sense anything other than the daze of death that can freeze a beloved's heart. In the beginning, even her son's plans for college, the dream she attached to all of her joy, the culmination of a lifetime of wanting, even this, when it was brought up by friends and church folk, was not enough to pull her up from her sadness.

Tree and Olivia, now a step beyond childhood, an unnoticed leap from daughters to mothers, searched for ways to mend the rip of grief that had opened up the heart of the woman they both loved. They steadied themselves on what they had already learned in taking care of Olivia's mother, using all that, plus quiet songs and Bible reading, in trying to take care of Tree's.

They cooked and cleaned. They spoke in whispers. They straightened Miss Nellie's sheets and blanket but did not wash them, arranged her closet and drawers. They dusted the furniture and neatly placed her slippers at the foot of the bed. And when Ruth would sleep-walk into her mother's room the young girls would ease her tired body into the pressed linens and comforting reminders that Miss Nellie had been there, slept there, loved there.

Together Tree and Olivia worked as a single unit caressing Ruth back into life. They searched for the spark within the mother's eyes and they fanned it with just enough care, blew upon it with just the right amount of lightness; and they moved in and out from house to house like an old married couple, finishing what the other one left standing.

They found ways of talking about Miss Nellie without abusing her memory, urging Ruth to move ahead without pushing her, keeping the grandmother's spirit alive without becoming morose. And because of their ferocity of tenderness, their unspoiled mercy, and the way they began and ended within one another, life started to breathe and grow once more inside Ruth's soul.

E. Saul threatened to defer his entrance into college under the guise of making sure his mother was going to be okay and no one but Olivia saw the glimmer in his eyes when he said it. She alone saw he was trying to use the tragedy to ease his desire into being and she did not betray his confidences.

After watching his sister and her friend, however, so selflessly abandon their girlish summer, sacrificing everything to bring Ruth through the storm of bereavement, he decided that what had been prayed by his mother must ultimately come to pass. And finally after bearing the brunt of his sister's anger and the stares of a stronger Ruth, he promised that he would go to school in the fall.

He could not help but see the stripped-away despair in his mother's eyes, the stretched but still desperate need for her son to leave Smoketown and make something of the Love name; and so he vowed that he would study subjects that were dignified and important and with careful attention to fulfilling their dreams, he would make his mother and his dead grandmother proud.

The months then from May to August passed gently and without event. Tree and Olivia spent the summer growing up in ways that only living in love can teach. They learned to make pies and jellies and how to save scraps and turn them into soup. They earned a little money begging chores from their neighbors, cleaning jars for canning, sorting through cluttered closets, collecting rags; and they combined their nickels and pennies to pay for goods and bills during the weeks that Ruth couldn't work.

They woke up early, beginning their errands without complaint; and they fell asleep just as the sun was dropping, their days and their nights filled up with living a woman's life. They laughed at the changes in their bodies, the loosening of their longings; and in between the hours of cleaning and earning pay, they dreamed great dreams for themselves.

They discovered that the push to grow up suited them, that they no longer needed the play and carefree days of childhood. They recognized the responsibility that was being placed upon both of them; but they realized that they actually preferred it to being little girls. Though they both missed Miss Nellie and the unsullied ways she nurtured them and even though they worried for Ruth and grew weary with Mattie, they found that the summer of a mother's grief was actually a welcomed passage of life.

E. Saul paid close attention to the changes in his sister and her friend. And he went about his own passage. He prepared for a life at college by selling all of his farm tools, digging up the bulbs and seeds of his childhood and selling them to farmers, and finally taking a job in a white lawyer's office, cleaning the shelves and filing away papers. And Ruth, watching the heartfelt determination of her son and the swift and easy maturity of her daughter, eventually pulled herself away from the grave and had, by the long days of July, discovered that she could spend an entire evening without the spill of tears.

On the inside looking out and on the outside looking in, all appeared to be well at the edge of Smoketown. The adolescence of two girls, the closing up of the wound of grief, and the emergence of a young black male scholar. But the evil had begun and while no one was measuring except an old woman who lived alone in the dark and abandoned forest, just in the midst of what appeared to be healing, it wrapped its second layer around bursting hearts.

Roy had been gone so long, more than two years, that Olivia had stopped sleeping with the light on. She quit biting her fingernails and was able to look a person in the eye without suddenly becoming anxious and turning away. She was more at ease around others, made better grades in school, and began to think of herself as lucky.

Even with the death of Miss Nellie and even with the imminent departure of her good friend, E. Saul, she felt light and slight of burden. Mattie remained bound to her bed, demonstrating an occasional flicker of life; but Olivia had even loosened her desperation that her mother not die. She had become convinced of her own skills and resources and was no longer afraid of being left alone.

She assumed that her brother would not return to Greensboro, to their house on the edge of Smoketown. His friends were all in the war, overseas, making heroes of themselves. Tootsie's Billiards closed when Red Foster got shot by a jealous husband. So Olivia, though spending most of her time with her best friend next door, cleaned out all of his clothes and moved into his room farther away from their mother who refused to die. She had not, in more than a year, considered that Roy would come home. Having laid that burden down, she never thought to warn anyone about him.

It was a solemn drive though not quiet for the young man as he hitched a ride from Fayetteville. Straight across sandy flat roads and into the dry foothills of the piedmont, the driver talked. A born-again Christian, he tried to get Roy to confess his sins and claim the promise of eternal life. Roy would not participate in the reading of a flimsy leaflet the driver pulled out of the glove compartment and would not even look at the man who drove him home. He kept his eyes on the road ahead of him acting as if he were the one doing the driving while the Bible-spouting pickup man begged, pleading for his redemption.

Roy got out at the main road, about six miles from his mother's house. Opened the door while the car was still moving and walked away to the words of the driver, "Christ be with you, brother."

Roy did not turn to the man who was unable to name the burden he felt while the sullen teenager rode beside him. And the driver pulled away, more relieved than Roy now that the shared journey was over.

For six hot miles the young man walked on common paths and wondered what he had done in coming home. Wondered what voice had beckoned him. And he stirred up familiar dust with the toes of his shoes, recognized farms and farmers and cars that passed; but he could not name the thought that brought him back to Smoketown.

Caked with the sweat and dirt of an August Carolina, Roy stepped into the house that sheltered his boyhood, went to the kitchen and found a bottle of booze. It was old, uncapped, high on a shelf near the door. It was where he always remembered the liquor to be. And he stood without a chair and reached for what he hoped might be left.

After two glasses he went into the room where his mother lay the day he had left. And as if nothing had passed between them, no time, no space, she twisted in the same position on the bed. Her body a fixture in the sheets.

He stood at the door just staring at her. Incapable of pity and certainly of love, he just watched. He thought how easy it would be to kill her and how that might just be the only kind thing he would ever do. He thought how she was nothing to him. How he heard stories of men who cried at the graves of their mothers. Tough, mean men who folded into babies when they would hear a song about somebody's mama, recalling a tender moment.

But for Hangman, there were no tender moments. No memories to keep, no stories to tell. It wasn't even that he hated her, thought she had treated him unfairly. There was only nothing; and sometimes he thought that was worse.

When the young black girl came into the house late in the afternoon before his sister had returned from her trip into town, Roy was not thinking of evil. The sun was high and relentless. The air, drained of lightness. But he was not angry from the heat. He was not remembering his mother or Candy or his sister or living on the edge of sorrow. He was not ciphering the cruelty of his own heart nor the damage he could do to the heart of a child.

He was drunk, sitting at the kitchen table playing with matches, toying with a flame, enjoying the danger of fire, seeing how long it would take before his skin would burn and blister.

She walked in as if it were her house, eased, innocent, and was startled at her neighbor's return. The look on her face, the fear, the surprise, it pleased him. It was the way he thought everyone looked at him. So to see it so clearly, so uninhibited, locked, took hold, fortified what he had always believed about himself.

"Hello, little Tree." Roy smiled and blew out the match that was burning in his hand. He had no plans of harm.

"Roy, I didn't know you were home," Tree stammered. "Is Olivia around?"

She felt uncomfortable and it showed in her voice, in the flight of her eyes.

"No." He smiled, pausing for a moment to enjoy the reaction his homecoming had provoked.

"But why don't you come in here and sit at the table with me and wait for her?" He pushed the chair out from under the table with his foot.

"Just tell her I came by." Tree had her hand on the knob of the door.

Roy jumped from his seat and moved between his next-door neighbor and her exit. He had not liked the way she arrived, comfortable and entitled, nor the way she was trying to depart, much too proudly and quickly.

"I said come and sit with me at the table."

And though he did not mean to press so deeply into the young girl's shoulder, he pushed her from the door into the chair at the table.

"I just want to talk. You can talk, can't you?"

And the girl nodded slowly.

"What grade you going in this year?" he asked, trying to lighten his voice and sound interested.

"Eighth," she said without facing him. The fear began to dry her throat. She thought she heard something, high-pitched and delicate, but she couldn't make it out.

"Eighth? My, but haven't you grown up?" He studied her, remembering her when she was smaller, less mature, thinking about his sister and how they had been friends for so long, how Olivia never bowed to the disapproval of the white children once she got to school.

"I probably should get home. E. Saul will be waiting. He's

leaving this weekend for college." She moved as if she was going to stand up.

"Sit down." His voice was angry and loud. "We're having a conversation. Aren't we having a conversation?"

The fury in Roy's voice startled Tree and she slowly dropped into her seat across from his.

Something changed. He could feel it. She could see it. She tried to think of something to say, something to lessen his focus on her, something to help her exit. But whatever had come apart in his mind was quickly unraveling in front of them.

"You don't walk away from someone when you're talking. Didn't you learn that in that farm school you niggers go to?"

He took a drink. Tree froze. She could not think of how to leave.

"So E. Saul's going to college, huh? That's just perfect," he said and downed another swallow.

When he turned the bottle up to his mouth, Tree focused on Roy and noticed his hands. They were not so strange. Not so different seeming. They just looked like hands. Fingers gripping and releasing. Knuckles tight and tall. Palms wet and slippery. Nails curved and smooth. And although they were white, she knew at the moment that he put down the bottle and grabbed for her neck that they were the father's hands that she had never been able to find.

There was that thought, a slight fluttering of wings leaving the air around them, and then nothing else.

It was not much of a struggle for Roy. When she screamed the first time and he slapped her, she did not make another noise. It was, in fact, almost too easy for him. He held her down, slammed her head into the floor, pinning her beneath him.

In only a period of a few seconds, even before he was sure of what he was going to do, he tore her open, and forced all of himself, the bitterness, the shame, the hatred, the anger, all of it he tried to cram into the young girl.

When he finished and rolled off of her, he glanced up to find his mother, having awakened and left her room. She stared at him, recognized him and what he had done, and then she fell back into the hallway.

Roy threw the empty bottle across the room, turned toward his mother's shadow, then down at the trembling, crying girl. He stood up, kicked her, and walked out the door.

Mattie's feeble attempt at resurrection was of no consequence. She left her bed because she smelled smoke, a familiar push to rouse her from her grave. She got up thinking of river water and birth. By the time she arrived at the door from the hall into the kitchen, her son's madness had ruptured, the spirit of a little girl had already slipped away; and she was too old and too sick and too late to do anything to stop it.

She recoiled at what she saw, lost herself in an evil she helped create, and did not regain consciousness until Olivia stood over her, shaking her with tremendous force, demanding to know the truth.

Mattie however knew nothing, especially nothing about a thing as deep and pure and penetrating as truth. She dropped her head and closed her eyes, her daughter cursing her to hell. And with that, a final and permanent choice of death for the weary woman and the snap in Olivia's mind, the evil wrapped its way around the third and final time.

Tree was cradled in her mother's arms, deaf and blind and mute. She was uprooted and cut away. Ruth, herself only recently alive, scrambled for something, everything, trying to bring her baby back to life. But the young girl was empty of anything, anything at all. Not bitterness, not hatred, not pain, not anything. She was wood, hollow and void, a limb floating in shallow water. And Ruth did not know how to care for such a thing so dead.

When E. Saul got home from work he could only grasp at pieces. From Ruth he could hear only terror and the primal anguish of a mother over her ripped and broken child. From his sister he saw only the bruises, the drops of blood that pooled across her neck, and a glaze across her eyes that seemed slowly to unsteady them.

When he faced the window that gave view to the house next door and saw Olivia storming from the house, a gleam of silver in her hand, he left his mother's side, his sister's fallen stare and emptied spirit, and headed after his neighbor.

He ran after her as she marched down the road, calling out her name to which she never responded, never heard. Once he caught up with her there was no discussion between the two of them, only a struggle just beyond the limits of Smoketown, just within sight of a patrol car that had stopped earlier to ask a young man walking a weaving path if he had some identification.

The eyewitness report as recorded in the next day's paper said a Negro boy was fighting with a white girl just at the edge of town, wrestling over a butcher knife. The deputy yelled at the boy to drop the weapon and then shot him twice in the chest without harming his apparent victim.

The sheriff's office had been quoted as saying that there were no future plans to investigate the incident any further. Everyone had agreed that force had been necessary and that the shooting had been justified, all within the legal bounds of the system. The boy's body was later released to an old woman, a Miss Comely, who arrived soon after it happened and claimed that she was a friend of the family.

The girl, the paper went on to report, was sedated and taken immediately to a state hospital for observation, obviously traumatized by the events of that late August night. She had no family or next of kin to contact.

Having no mother, since Mattie had now finally mastered the art of dying, her best friend and neighbor gone without a forwarding address, her brother escaped, her life consumed by evil, Olivia, a young girl who was becoming a woman, would stay locked up and forgotten for a very long time.

Years later when folks would ask the residents of Smoketown about the two little houses that marked the line between black and white, the two little houses that stood so close together but bore witness to worlds apart, the two little houses that no one, black or white, would rent or buy, people would shake their heads, peer toward the graveyard behind a little brick church, and out toward the headstone of a woman who used to hear angels.

They would remember a warm spring day and wearing a look of pride that one of their own had managed a way out of the sorrow. They would think of that Kingdom of God Banquet and the perfect way a mother loved her son and how everything, for the first time in their lives, had felt exactly right. They would consider their own shame in having let their guards down so easily and so low. They would look at the grave of Miss Nellie Star Broadnax Blackwell and they would quietly shake their heads and say that they should have known.

And even though they had not ever allowed themselves to be so full and happy again, never ate that much or laughed that loud. Even though they now counted the deaths of neighbors and asked about last words and the rooms where people had died, checked to see if the eyes of the dead one were opened or closed and calculated what day of the week the person had passed, even though they never got so spirited about the accomplishments of another young person from Smoketown, the price had already been paid, it had been too late.

Evil, in its triune and ugly face, had warned them and they had not heeded its counsel.

March 15, 1960

This hereby orders the release of Olivia Ruth Jacobs from the Long Memorial Mental Hospital. She is released into her own custody after having been institutionalized for a number of years due to severe depression.

This release is ordered by the Clerk of Court for the State of North Carolina and the Guilford County Offices for Mental Health.

Signed,
Dr. Lindsey Pope
Chief of Psychiatry
Long Memorial Mental Hospital

Nine

The new chief of medicine at the mental hospital took inventory of all the files in the facility. He started with the records of those patients who had been in the hospital the longest, proceeded to those of the most newly committed patients, and ended with the files locked in cabinets down behind the basement stairs that were marked in bold black ink, DECEASED.

In 1960, the state government hired Dr. Pope because of his tight administrative style and because of a decision to clean house in the state hospitals, beginning with the psychiatric facility that was slated to close by the year 1965. The funds were low and the state senate was demanding a new, streamlined means of managing mental illness. Those patients who had lived in the facility for more than ten years and who could be diagnosed as being functional enough to be placed into a productive, tax-paying existence were quickly discharged and released.

Olivia Jacobs was twenty-eight years old and had lived at

Long's for fifteen years. She was originally classified as catatonic, uncommunicative, and mentally unstable due to severe trauma. For the first five years of her commitment, she was considered a suicide risk and was housed in the ward with thirty other female patients who were tied to their beds at night, kept locked in tiny cells, and were allowed only thirty minutes outside every day.

Later she would recall that she had never experienced this mode of treatment as confining or unpleasant. She hardly remembered those five years at all.

When she turned eighteen, they transferred her into a room with five other patients; and her records reflect that she began to register activity around her by following the other girls with her eyes and demonstrating emotion through facial expressions and the grip and release of fisted hands. She rarely, however, participated in group activities, preferring instead to stay alone, reading, in her bed. She was given several electric shock treatments; and although the doctors had been optimistic about the outcome, there were no behavorial changes.

At age twenty-one, she spoke for the first time since she had been committed. A new patient, a young female, fourteen, was being assaulted by three other girls. Olivia first began banging her book along the railing of her bed and when no one came, she screamed for help.

For the last seven years that she was institutionalized she spoke only four more times. Once to say good-bye to a nurse of whom she had become fond and who was leaving to get married. Once to reply with the word "no" when she was asked if she knew if any of her family were still alive. Once in a conversation with a blind boy that no one else heard but in which she told him the color of the sky at dusk. And finally at her exit interview that was supervised by Dr. Pope and attended by Dr. Levi, her psychiatrist of ten years, two nurses, and a secretary who took notes in a short, fat binder in which the pages were held together by three silver rings.

Dr. Pope began the interview. "Olivia Jacobs, age twenty-eight, female, committed to the facility in August, 1945." He peered over the folder at the young patient.

Olivia was staring at the table. Her hair was swept back in a tight ponytail and she was wearing a blue flowered gown.

"It says here that you were brought to the hospital when you were thirteen." He flipped through the pages in her chart. "Your mother died then?" he asked.

The doctors and the nurses and the recording secretary all peered at Olivia. She didn't answer.

Dr. Levi cleared his throat. "She was a victim of assault." He turned toward his patient, a sympathetic glance, confident that he had correctly ordered her history and diagnosed her condition.

"I see," the chief of psychiatry replied. "And she hasn't spoken since a time of distress when a roommate was being beaten up?"

One of the nurses, the old one, the one who seemed to know her best, Miss Alice Spears, answered. "She's said a few things since then."

She reached over and patted the young woman on the hand. "But mostly, no, she's remained quiet."

The secretary furiously wrote down what was being said.

"And, Miss Jacobs, do you understand that we're planning to release you?"

Olivia felt the nurse's hand on hers. She liked how it felt to be touched by the older woman, the comfort and care that was implied. She didn't respond to the chief doctor. She thought he was brusque and unhappy.

"Olivia, Miss Jacobs, you've been in here a long time, a lot of years, isn't there somewhere you'd like to go?"

She still did not answer.

"Make a note that the patient does not respond," Dr. Pope said to the secretary.

The woman with the binder blew out a puff of air and kept writing.

"Well, there's no reason for you to stay here," he said. "Even if you don't talk, we're going to have to let you go." He closed the file and wrote something on the top.

Dr. Levi drew a line through Olivia's name that was written somewhere near the bottom of his writing pad. He had lost ten patients already that day.

"Thank you," was all she said as she got up from the table, gathered up her things, and left the meeting.

The next day she was released from the hospital with two sets of clothes that were donated by the Church Women's Society, one pair of shoes, black ankle boots that were a size too small, fourteen dollars, and a seed of life growing in her womb.

She walked away, turning back only once to notice the window where she had sat when she first noticed the bright orange sunset that faded into thin, narrow wisps of purple clouds and which she had reported to the boy who had not asked but in whom she recognized a desire to know.

She was discharged from the institution and three months pregnant by the unseeing boy whose name she never learned. Neither she nor the nurses nor the supervising physician bothered to check for such an unlikely thing at the time of her departure.

She left the hospital aware of something moving within her, thinking that something had broken inside of her; but she had not considered it could be a growing, emerging life. Like her mother before her, Olivia rejected the notion that she could be pregnant since everything within her felt old and lost and dead.

She took a bus to Virginia and settled into the Salvation Army Women's Shelter in Danville. She swept the floors and changed the linens; and months later after having given birth to a quiet, slow-moving baby who followed her mother with her eyes, she tried to think of tenderness, tried to dream again.

The young babe, the stirring of grace, and the limping along of hope, almost succeeded. But once the child was old enough to ask her questions and call attention to the long life of disappearance she had lived, the sorrow and the memory of something held and lost poured across Olivia's mind and won out.

She left her child because she was confident that everything she could share had been ripped up and burned like the church across the street from her birth house in Smoketown, that everything she would give her would be tainted, sullied, and unlovely.

She was sure the little girl could learn life more easily from someplace else, from anybody else. So, after coming home from work one day and realizing that she was pretending to be more than she was, pretending to have more than she had, she packed her daughter a small bag with some clothes and a toy, pinned five dollars to the inside front pocket in her bib overalls, and dropped her off one last time at Miss Kathy's Play Care Center. She walked away, convincing herself that she had done the right thing.

It hurt, but no more than the long windy nights when she thought she heard the muffled cries of her best friend, Tree. Or when she reached into her Bible and pulled out a loose-leaf paper with a poem from E. Saul's hand. Or when she happened upon little girls whispering a secret that toppled them over in laughter. There were times she was sure she would not breathe again. And yet, she always did. In and out. Labored and listless, Olivia breathed and lived, her sadness an old coat she never took off.

So that many years later, when she woke up from a dream about pine trees dancing under a summer sky and she finally decided to search for her daughter, the story was so tired and the sorrow so deliberate, she wasn't sure of why she wanted to find her, what she would say once they discovered one another, nor how she would explain where and what she had been.

For once, however, in her long and sleepwalking existence, she lifted herself above the memories and beyond the agonizing losses, pulled herself away from the pitch of despair, and fought and scratched all the way back to the ghosts of Smoke-town.

It was a journey of low-lying hopefulness but she did not turn from it and run away. She pushed herself all the way there. What or rather who she found untangled the tight knots and opened a space in her lungs to breathe.

She died while growing back her heart.

Epilogue

Just after Anna had been born, a nurse brought her in for me to feed her. She was so tiny in that woman's arms, so helpless and pink and frail. The nurse showed me how to position the baby across my chest, how to place the nipple in her little mouth, how to angle her head and steady her neck. I was nervous and tired, weary after a very long time of labor, and I couldn't get my milk to come out.

The nurse was angry at me. I guess she was tired too. She would raise her voice, "Sit up, lean back, hold her beneath you," growing louder and more impatient with each instruction.

I tried to do everything she ordered me to do. I changed positions, held my body differently, tried to relax; but nothing would come out. Even as Anna took the nipple, clearly doing her part, it seemed as if I were as dry as a bone, as if I had nothing inside myself to give to her. Even though I felt the presence of the milk, even though I thought I had what she needed contained in my full, tender breasts, I was unable to pass it on.

The nurse sighed heavily, sweeping Anna from my arms in one swift motion. "We'll try again later," she huffed. "In the meantime," she added in a disappointed tone as she headed to the door with my daughter, "try to calm down. This ain't rocket science, you're just feeding your baby. It's the easiest thing you'll do as a mother."

She left the room and I was completely alone. Suddenly I began to cry and it was as if I became a river. Tides of old tears swelled and burst. Wave after wave bumped and rolled across me. I ached from the sheer force of so much emotion streaming from inside me that I thought I would surely drown in this unmanaged sorrow. My heart split and opened like another ready womb.

I did not know how to be a mother. I did not think I was capable of such a role, such a relationship. I had no island of memory, no foundation of wisdom within me. I had no place to go. And I wasn't sure I should even try.

Perhaps, I thought in my drowning moment, I did not have what my daughter must have and that maybe I should rise from my bed of labor and delivery and quickly exit from her life. Before she was spoiled. Before her life was corrupted by all that I was and all that I was not. Before I so gravely disappointed her.

And it was just beyond that moment, just outside its coming and going, just after I choked and breathed, that I thought of and consequently forgave my mother. I had not expected such a thing, imagined such a development of birth. But it happened. In just a brief, tiny tick of a clock, I suddenly understood her fear, her hesitation, her choice. And the resentment and bitterness, at least for that moment, were gone.

When the nurse brought Anna to me the second time and slipped her next to my heart, the milk flowed heavily and with ease. My daughter took all that she could. My breast became the source of her life. And when the nurse came back for my baby, to return her to the nursery, I slept, for the first night in a very long time, in peace.

I close Olivia's book, resting it against my chest, surprised by the memory from my daughter's birth. It was not the answer I seek, not the story I am trying to find, and I don't know why it is that now I would remember the clean easy flow of milk that poured from my breast or that delicate moment of forgiveness.

I don't understand why it is in this place, this unfamiliar and unrelated place, that I would recall the way it felt to have my daughter next to me, that I would remember such a moment of grace and hope. That I would recall how it is to be in perfect love.

I lean my head and shoulders against that old velvet rocking chair and close my eyes and remember something else, an old thing, a forgotten thing, a Sunday afternoon when I was bathed in sweetness and a picture I had drawn when I was seven years old.

It was late in the summer and I was living in the home of a preacher and his wife. I remember that there were lots of children, that I couldn't tell who was real and who wasn't, that we were all treated the same, no one more or less special than the next one. I remember that for the six or eight months I stayed there I slept long full nights, that my stomach never ached, that I played board games and cards without asking to sit so I could face the door. I remember that the house was cool and spacious, that the windows were always open, and that big noisy fans blew in every room.

It was after church, early in the afternoon, and we were all sitting around the table just about to enjoy our lunch. The father, a big man who wore a thick gray suit every Sunday and who hugged so tightly you'd lose your breath, stood to say grace as he did at every meal.

"Children," he said, and we knew that was our cue to reach out and hold each other's hands. "God loves you more than you will ever know, more than you've been despised or mistreated, more than you think is possible. And even if you've been hurt or even if you're going to be hurt, it cannot bind you or hold you or keep you in the way that God's love is able."

The preacher smiled, his eyes, wide with delight. He lifted his hands and unfolded his fingers. He was as big as a mountain.

"God reached down from the gates of heaven and set this world to spinning. He loved it when he made it, 'cause he knew it started in goodness, and he loved it when he realized it would not always stay so. He loved it so much that he planted himself in every thing he made. Hill and glen, planet and shooting star, little bitty drops of water and perfect flakes of snow, lacy petals of soft flowers, and . . ." He cleared his throat and we all listened; we were all so hungry for something to fill up the emptiness.

"And in you." He paused just for a moment and I felt the shock of good news. Even at the young age of seven I knew I was desperate for salvation.

"God has planted himself in you."

I became so light-headed that I fell against my chair; and the room exploded into colors, yellow and orange and a red so bright it covered over every dull imagining or dim thought I had ever known. When I came to, the big preacher and his wife were kneeling over me, dark, loving hands stroking my brow. I was trembly and weak; but I was alert with the knowledge that something had opened inside of me, something slipped and made room for more than just my loss, more than just my sorrow. I somehow understood that I would one day survive my loneliness and that at that moment, the only regret I felt and could name was that my mother had not received the same stern blessing.

Later that evening I sat at the kitchen table in that cool, restful house and drew pictures of a tree. Tall, full, stretching to heaven but firmly rooted on earth, thick limbs, big, brown branches, filled with smiling, laughing children. It was, I knew at the time, the most important picture I had ever drawn.

"What you got there, baby girl?" The preacher sat down beside me. I could feel the warmth of his breath on my neck.

"It's God," I answered.

The preacher nodded, the smile spread across his face. "And who's that?" he asked, pointing to a little girl just in the crook of a limb, alone but still steady, still safe.

"That's me," I answered, sounding as if I thought he should have guessed that.

"Ah," he responded in perfect understanding, "there you are, way up close in the arms of God." He pulled me to him and squeezed and I remember thinking that God Himself could not hold me any tighter.

I sit in the breezy room where my mother sorted through her life and I think of that picture I drew when I was too young even to understand what was happening. I think of that scared, abandoned, little girl and that clear, undeniable moment when she was not afraid.

I think of a preacher who opened himself so completely to lost children and a woman who lived her life bound to her sadness but who, just before passing over to another life, to the next one, happier I hope, reached back, searching even in the bowels of her hell, and found me.

I realize as I sit in the place where she grieved and dreamed that I had been wrong. We are more than just pieces yanked away and given to another, more than just bits broken off and lost. We are more than an incomplete puzzle. For even if we merely brush against one another, two strangers speaking a word of kindness on a warm afternoon, two people laughing at the same cartoon, even if we forget where it was we met or never even learn each other's name, even if we are mother and daughter who were pulled apart only seconds after we became two instead of one, or even if we were friends taken from each other by someone else's violence, we are forever bound together, forever related, forever connected.

Once we have met and touched, once our lives have intersected, even in the smallest way, even if only in a dream or only in the picture of a child, we are instantly joined together, like a dance that never ends, like a tree with full and limber branches, like the arms of God. And for good or for bad, the connection will bind or will loose, sometimes doing both.

In my mother's album there are only a few clues to what her life had been. A photograph of a family, one black, one white, three women, two girls, two boys, a note on the back that read *Easter in Smoketown,* poems written in longhand, authored by someone with the initials E.S., a letter from the military about someone named Roy, a relative I presume, and a release form from a mental hospital.

There are a couple of obituaries, silly rhymes and riddles, and an article from the forties that had been ripped and taped together about an incident involving my mother and a young black boy, the same one in the picture, an incident that sent her to the asylum for an indefinite time. There are a few more pictures, mostly of me when I was a little girl, a curl of hair, mine, I guess, a copy of a psalm, and a poem about a tree.

And this is all that I have of her. This and the sense that she was broken a very long time ago. Sliced and rent in such a way that she was not able to give love again. Bear a child maybe. Watch from a distance. Live and work through endless days of mediocrity. But not give love, not open up herself.

I realize, however, as I shut the lid on the old box and head down the stairs, I have what I have, a trunk, a scrapbook, a few tender memories of her last three weeks on earth, and a daughter who birthed in me forgiveness. And I will carry these things and cherish them, because they are the parts of my mother connecting me to her and drawing me to my daughter, interlacing me with all the other people I have known.

As I gather up my mother's things and carry them to my car, as I place the trunk in the seat next to mine, Olivia's clothes, shoes, and personal items in the back, I turn to the house and the window where I am sure my mother used to sit. Then my eyes drop down and I notice that the landlord is outside, sitting on the porch, rocking in one of the two chairs. She looks out toward the road as an old brown Chevrolet pulls up behind me. I watch the familiar old man as he opens the car door, slides from behind the wheel, steps out, and waves in my direction.

Across the yard, between the branches of the corner sugarberry, I turn back toward the rocking chair and I see the landlord's dark face, her silver hair, the split vision she possesses. I wait to see if she has something to say to me, a question to ask, a greeting to share. And for what seems like a long time, seconds stretched into a lifetime, she and the man at the car just look at me, just watch me from their distances.

As I see her, see her seeing me, her eyes now suddenly steady, like bark, I am reminded of something my mother said at a meal we shared last week. It was one of the few times in the twenty days we were together that she spoke more than just a few words.

Anna had come home from school that afternoon, angry at her best friend, a friend that she had known since she was six and a first-grader at Ashton Elementary.

Lateesha moved with her family into our neighborhood when she, like Anna, was only a toddler. I met the little girl's mother one afternoon when we were both out enjoying a walk, our daughters strapped tightly in their strollers. We hit it off, became friends, and the girls became inseparable. Anna adores Lateesha.

My daughter sat down at the dinner table, her eyes swollen and red. She slumped in her chair, took her fork, and began picking at her food.

"Do you want to talk about what happened?" I asked as I served Olivia. Having only been home an hour, I knew none of the details of the argument.

She shook her head.

"Do you want me to call her mother and the four of us work this out together?"

She rolled her eyes, put down her fork, and folded her arms hard across her chest.

I sat in my chair, placed the napkin across my lap, and started eating.

Dinner was leftovers. Vegetable lasagne from a potluck at work, salad, and fresh rolls that I brought home from the bakery next to the school. They were Anna's favorite.

She still had not taken a bite; and for a while, the three of us just sat quietly. I noticed that Olivia had stopped eating and had bowed her head. For a minute, I thought she was praying.

"I had someone once," she said, "a friend." And when she spoke, she startled both Anna and myself.

"She was the only person . . ." Her voice trailed off and she didn't finish her sentence.

Anna glanced up, checking my reaction, waiting for me to respond. I stuffed some salad in my mouth and raised my eyebrows.

There was a pause. Olivia still faced the table.

"That was a long, long time ago," she said.

Then it seemed forever before she spoke again. I could feel my daughter's concentration.

"But sometimes even those things you think are dead, pulled up by the roots and cast aside, sometimes even what you know is lost forever, shows up, real and breathing, like a dead man in the garden."

I stopped chewing my lettuce. I turned to Anna who was watching my mother, her grandmother. I followed her eyes and watched her too.

One lone tear rolled down the old woman's cheek. One single drop of water, and Anna and I looked with a bit of embarrassment as she reached with her napkin and wiped it away before it slid down her chin.

I quickly turned away. Anna picked up her fork and ate.

The dinner ended without further conversation. Anna left the room and called her friend, to set things right, I imagined. Olivia and I cleaned the dishes and then sat in silence as I phoned and we waited for her ride.

I must admit that at the time she spoke, I thought that she was talking about me. That she was talking about finding me, that I was the one who had been found. That I was the dead thing that was now alive, that I was the one for whom she wept that single tear. And I waited the entire rest of the evening, hoping for her confirmation.

All she said, however, was good-bye, which she spoke softly to both my daughter and me as she walked out on the porch and down to the driver, who waved as he got out and opened her door.

Later that night I fell asleep, still not understanding what my mother had meant. It became simply one more riddle left unsolved.

Until now.

As the sun stretches across the early afternoon sky and as I stand next to the car, my mother's life neatly ordered and stacked on the seats, I recognize from that gaze with the old woman on the porch, in that silent exchange of vision, that she bears some of the secrets my mother never named. That she was more than just a landlord, more than just a woman in whose house my mother lived, more than just some passing acquaintance.

She was my mother's friend; she was that only person. She

was the one who was yanked up by the roots and given to the wind, the one who had broken free from death and had become my mother's final resting place. She was the source of my mother's courage to find me, and the strength finally to put all the ghosts away.

The old woman simply lifts her head like it is the end of an unspoken prayer. She turns away from me and toward the man parked behind me, her brother, I presume, and nods as if she knows that I understand.

Then, just as quickly as she came forward, she rocks back and slips away, her dark brown eyes, the strong, steady gaze, broken but not lost.